THE POLICE CALLED IT
AN ACCIDENT . . .

Sir Robert Cassillis did not believe that his neighbor had taken a fatal fall by chance. But before he could prove his suspicions, he himself met an untimely death.

It was up to the inquisitive Dr. Davie to follow the thread of the mystery . . . into the intimate lives of Tidwell's most eminent citizens . . . into the heart of a deadly conspiracy . . . and into the lair of an unscrupulous killer.

. . . BUT DAVIE CALLED IT
MURDER!

Murder Ink.® Mysteries

Scene Of The Crime™ Mysteries

A *Murder Ink.®* Mystery

NO CASE FOR
THE POLICE

V. C. Clinton-Baddeley

A DELL BOOK

FOR FRIENDS IN AMERICA
C. C. & BEECHER HOGAN

Published by
Dell Publishing Co., Inc.
1 Dag Hammarskjold Plaza
New York, New York 10017

ISBN: 0-440-16424-9

Reprinted by arrangement with
William Morrow and Company, Inc.
Printed in the United States of America
First Dell printing—January 1982

ONE

I

Suddenly the road tipped down between the pine trees. Leaving the foxgloves behind, the bus had started its descent towards the village. The distant glimpses of the sea disappeared behind the shoulder of the valley. As he crossed the railway bridge—the disused line already overgrown, the sandstone cutting more than ever mysterious—Davie knew that he was home.

First the pine woods, then the beech woods. And then, as the road levelled out at the bottom of the hill, the first houses, and a sign which bade the visitor "Welcome to Tidwell St. Peter's."

Davie wondered a little about that. As he remembered the village, visitors had never been in the least welcome—except to those who catered for them. Sixty years back, when the motor car had been a rarity and the airplane unknown, the place had been a jealously preserved haunt of retired colonels and demoted memsahibs, who, leaving behind them a life of oriental splendour, of turbaned servants, elephants who raised a military trunk to the right people, tiger hunts, polo, tennis, amateur theatricals at Simla, had somehow contrived in more straitened circumstances to live a life of dignity among the pine trees and rhododendrons, still largely concerned beneath softer skies with the propulsion of balls, golf, tennis, cricket and croquet. Indeed the more whimsical ones, inspired by legends of Drake, obtained some mastery over the biassed wood. Tidwell St. Peter's is still a place of retirement for the distinguished old, and in varying parts of the parish a variety of balls still smack, click, or thud, over or into the net, the marshes, the bunker, the gorse and the heather. But backgrounds are different. There are fewer memories now of Naini Tal and Peshawar, more of Manchester and Golders Green.

And now there were houses and gardens on both sides of the road, and presently the golf links on the right and a pine wood on the left, and then the road dipped down again for the final descent to the sea.

Of course it *was* altered: there were more houses, but not many, and most of the old houses seemed to be still there, though a few had been pulled down and replaced by flats; and there, on the right, was the Nursery Garden exactly as it always had been.

That turning to the left led to Davie's old home. You could not see it from the main road, but he had not the smallest difficulty in seeing himself sixty, sixty-five, years back, wandering along in a holland pinafore, and not the slightest risk of being knocked down by anything.

More houses and more gardens—the steep hill of terraced houses to the right—and then the bus turned sharply to the left by the great ilex tree (still there! he had never hoped for that), and came to a stop by the village hall. It was the end of the run, and the passengers spilled out upon the pavement. Davie was last. He had recognized nobody. It was the place that had come to meet him, after twenty years.

For a few seconds he waited there, looking about him. Across the road stood the rival hall, the Gospel Hall, red brick, unadorned, not a slate out of place, not a laurel leaf missing. Dear God! How those Brethren used to sing! Long ago, as a prejudiced son of the Anglican Church, Davie had thought them comical, those earnest voices yearning for the new Jerusalem. He did not think so now.

Picking up his case, he crossed the road, walked back a hundred yards, and turned left into the village street. It was already early evening and few people were about as he made his way along the pavement, the declining sun at his back, his long shadow (in the words of the liturgy) "preventing" him. "Prevent and follow us, O Lord"; what had the monkeys of revisers made of that one, he wondered, and stopped in front of a glossy vegetable shop with mendacious little plastic tickets all over the place saying "Specially Selected" and "Fresh Today." Now that was a change for the worse. This was the shop, the very shop, where old Mrs. Veitch and her two daughters had kept their glorious muddle of vegetables, and moreover had dispensed those bottles of lemonade which used to be stoppered with glass marbles. You had to push them down with a special opener, and if you had not got a special opener, then you had to do it with your thumb, or if you weren't very old, you had to ask Mrs. Veitch to do it for you, which meant carrying the bottle very carefully to the beach. Did any such bottles still exist, Davie wondered, a bottle with a pale green translucent marble in it?

Or was that just another thing lost to history? Those were the things that museums ought to collect while they could—but they rarely did. The fuss when some-one finds an Elizabethan bottle! Well, then . . .

A passing car, reflected in the window glass, re-called him to the present. Mrs. Veitch had been dead these thirty years; at the back of the shop he could see tins of Coca-Cola.

Turning away from the window, he went on down the pavement, and there was the garage on the left, and further on, on the right, the Ottery Arms, dolled up a bit, bigger, but essentially the same. He crossed the road, crossed the forecourt, and mounted the steps. He had arrived.

Fifteen minutes later, having signed his name and found his room, he walked across the garden to the path on the edge of the low cliff—low here but, on the right, mounting steeply to the beacon.

Below, in the great circle of the bay, lay the beach —the famous stone beach.

Once upon a time a grassy slope had stretched down nearly to the sea, but early in the nineteenth cen-tury, as a result of a tremendous storm, these stones had arrived from somewhere beneath the English Channel—round, flat stones as big as an open hand, quite unlike any other stones in neighbouring bays. The people of Tidwell St. Peter's used them to build their garden walls, to edge their flower beds, or sin-gly as doorstops. They were only to be found on the beach. They were not in the sandstone cliffs or inland in the dark red earth. More than anything else, it was this beach which had preserved the village from the tripper. You can't run races, play cricket, or wield a bucket and spade on stones. It was not the people so much as the place itself that was exclusive.

Davie turned to the left and wandered along the path towards the parade. Presently he reached the broad sea wall with the endpiece shaped like a mushroom. Children had run along the top of it these hundred years. A famous wall it was, too, immortalized by Ambrose Faddle, A.R.A., in that endlessly popular picture "Sons of the Sea," in which four early Victorian fisher boys sit dangling provocative toes, listening to an old salt telling the story of Trafalgar. "Sons of the Sea" had been exhibited at the Academy in 1880, but dates of that sort are not worth anyone's verification, and several aged fishermen, but not as aged as that, were in the habit of claiming that they had been the original models. All of which was splendid nonsense. Yet anyone who knew the aboriginal families of Tidwell St. Peter's could easily trace likenesses. George Pengelly who worked at the garage was exactly like the long-faced boy on the left of Ambrose Faddle's masterpiece. Likely indeed that the boy had been George's grandfather.

Davie sat down on one of the green benches and looked across the parade at the beach. Boats, lobster pots, ropes, windlasses, discreet rows of bathing cabins. A few late bathers. Gulls. Everywhere the gulls. And out in the tranquil bay two small boats. It was nearly all as he remembered it—except for one thing. Long ago there had been six bathing machines. "Machines"—no one had thought anything odd about that eighteenth century word, and they were indeed eighteenth century conceptions with two great wheels, originally intended to be drawn down to the sea by a horse. From precisely such a machine had George III entered the sea at Weymouth while the town band in a neighbouring machine played "God Save the King," appropriate music for the royal adventure. Those machines, blue and white, had adorned the beach at Tidwell St. Peter's for years. And now they were gone. But what had happened to them? It was his usual grumble: a "machine," a genuine piece of social history, gone with the tide.

Sixty years back Davie could see himself bathing from a machine with Robert.

Robert. Familiar sights had diverted his thoughts during the last half hour. But truly Robert was connected with all of them. Robert in the bathing machine, slim and brown. Robert in the sea, clean as a fish. Robert in his blue jersey. It had always been a blue jersey. He had been wearing a blue jersey that day he had taken Davie for a ride in his grandmother's Bath chair—that three-wheeled basketwork affair. You don't see them today, or do you still in Bath? They had taken it to the top of Clumber Rise, whence, ignorant of mechanical laws, they had coasted downhill at gathering speed and ended in the ditch. Robert's grandmother had been very angry, but more on account of damage to her Bath chair than of damage to her grandson.

Robert—chief figure in Davie's early memory. Robert, pouring his cod liver oil out of the window: Robert, with the aid of a gas jet, inducing an unbelievable (and unbelieved) temperature of 110 degrees: Robert, letting off a depth charge in the lake at Cadleigh, and accidentally sinking Miss Manger, ninth and last of Robert's governesses. Davie could see Miss Manger now, emerging from the lake like Aphrodite from the wave, a water lily in her streaming hair.

Robert climbing trees; Robert shooting rabbits; Robert in the pine wood, imparting to an astonished Davie (aged twelve) his earliest misinformation on the facts of life. Davie had been critical. Certainly the navel did not appear to unscrew. "Men's don't," Robert had said darkly, and Davie had not been able to answer that one.

Robert.

Suddenly it seemed cold. The sun was behind the hill. The bathers had left the water. Davie glanced at his watch; it was past seven. For a few more minutes he sat there staring at the sea. Then, still thinking about Robert, he made his way back along the cliff path to the hotel. Near the garden railing a child was throwing bits of bread to a flying circus of immaculate gulls.

Davie opened the gate and walked down the path between the roses.

The door to the sun lounge stood wide. On a glass-topped table an evening paper lay open at the gossip column—the column signed by "Westminster," that pseudonymous, repulsively familiar, multiple "I," who cherishes so many inaccurate anecdotes of so many famous people. "I remember an entertaining story of the late Sir Robert Cassillis," Westminster began.

Davie lowered himself into a deep chair and hailed a passing waiter. "A single whisky and water, please." But to his heart he said, "That hack remembers an entertaining story of the late Sir Robert Cassillis, does he? . . . I remember a hundred."

II

A hundred stories—but they were nearly all of young
Robert, Robert of the blue jersey, Robert at school,
Robert at Cambridge. After that their ways had
parted. Davie had stayed at Cambridge, Robert had
sought the furthest corners of the earth, engaged at
first in ministering to an empire. But Robert Cassillis
could never endure to be commanded. He had a
famous will, a famous temper, and an earnest need
to discover the answer to certain cherished questions.
In this age that kind of man climbs mountains or
seeks the polar regions, supported morally by govern-
ments, financially by newspapers, and miraculously
by radio. Robert Cassillis created a legend by doing
things in the manner of another century. He had a
mysterious gift for disappearing: for crossing deserts,
for losing himself in jungles, for hobnobbing with
headhunters in Borneo, or Tibetan monks in moun-
tain fastnesses. By the time he was forty the newspapers were comparing him with Sir Richard Burton.
Equally men of wit, mystery, and dangerous temper,
both had risked death. Burton perhaps, Cassillis certainly, had seen the shedding of blood. It had not
been his own.

And so, during more than forty years—Robert usually somewhere in Asia, Davie usually somewhere in
Europe—they who had lived in each other's pockets
had met only on rare occasions. Neither had altered
in his affection for the other, but inevitably something had been lost. Like the piano, friendship needs

practice. And then there had come a time when Robert had brought back a wife, and Davie, who knew a dragon when he saw one, had realized that three was very poor company indeed.

Ethel Cassillis was a snob and she was jealous. At a party she always kept her husband in view and if he talked to anyone too long, and particularly if he appeared to be enjoying himself, she would make a point of crossing the room and breaking the association up by the simple act of joining it. Nor was it only a matter of designing and dangerous women. Ethel was equally jealous of men, and specially of old friends. Davie she had regarded with a very jaundiced eye. She did not understand his little jokes, and so she always spoke of him with gay, defensive sarcasm. "Your friend, the professor," she would begin. "Not a professor." "Isn't he? He behaves like one. Poor me! I'm afraid I can't compete at all."

Nobody had ever understood why Robert had married Ethel, and everyone was properly sympathetic but secretly relieved when she walked off the end of a jetty one night and got herself drowned somewhere among the Greek islands. In most people's opinions Ethel Cassillis had led Robert a life. But your true lady-lover never profits by experience. If he is rid of one bondage, predictably and inevitably he looks around for another. Robert had found Irene.

Davie had met Irene two or three times in London. Gentle and sweet, she seemed a lovely wife for any man. But she was thirty and Robert was seventy. It didn't seem right—not for that particular sort of woman. It didn't seem safe: how could she be satisfied with a man of Robert's age? And yet it had worked. Robert had been entirely happy. They had made a year's honeymoon, going round the world, and then at last they had come home—home to Cadleigh Abbey, that lovely relic of Tudor avarice, looking down through rhododendron glades to willows weeping by the lily lake where Robert had torpedoed Miss Manger nearly sixty years before. It had seemed a right retirement from a brilliant life. But now, only six months later, that life was ended. Unless she were to produce a posthumous heir (and Davie had no information about that) the estate would go to a cousin; but, even so, Irene would be rich.

That much he reviewed in his mind as he drank his whisky. The rest of the story he had still to discover. All he knew was that the funeral was tomorrow, and that he was Robert's literary executor and would have to go through his papers.

He heaved himself out of his chair and entered the dining room. There was much to be said for a good hotel in a small seaside village. Lobsters, for instance. A lobster caught out there in the bay.

And when it came it was just as it ought to be. Even the mayonnaise was right. He had feared it would be bottled varnish—but no, it was genuine oil and authentic egg yolks; it had even been made with lemon juice instead of beastly vinegar.

Davie awarded the Ottery Arms three stars on the spot.

III

Half an hour later he was sitting in the outer lounge, the glass-fronted affair that gives on to the garden, watching his fellow visitors, hunched in basket chairs around glass-topped tables, drinking their ritual cups of coffee. Bad for the digestion, bad for sleep, but the correct thing to do. Everyone was very old, he noticed. Nowadays the young go hitchhiking across Europe. It was July, almost the high season, and the average age of the visitors was about sixty-five. It would not be long before they closed their novels, laid down their copies of *The Illustrated London News*, rolled up their knitting, and tottered either to the television room or gratefully to bed. Davie could do neither. He was expecting a visitor. "Forgive me if I do not say more," Irene had written. "Donald will call on you after dinner." Donald? Davie had no idea who Donald might be, but he sounded young—if he had been older Irene would have said "Donald X," or "my cousin, Colonel X"—but Donald, just Donald, was surely a young man.

While he waited he lost himself among the advertisements of *Country Life*. Should he buy Maple Barton for £40,000 with ten acres and ample stabling? Or would he be wiser to pay—it did not say what—for Moss Hall, an "imposing Georgian Residence with extensive views over park-like grounds"? "Park-like" was an interesting word. If the grounds were like a park why were they not precisely that—a park? In the end he decided to buy Clob Manor for £30,000 partly because of the name, partly because of the Adam decorations. And just as he had got that nicely fixed, he heard the porter saying in the doorway, "That's Dr. Davie over there, sir."

Davie had been right about a young man. Donald was somewhere in his twenties, tall and dark and hazel-eyed. He was wearing jeans and a royal blue polo-necked jumper.

Davie rose to meet him and signalled to the porter to wait.

"You are Donald, I expect," said Davie. "I'm sorry, but I don't know the rest of it."

"Bride. Donald Bride."

"The first thing is what will you drink?"

"Thank you. What are you drinking?"

"I am a victim of the demon whisky myself," said Davie, "but you—"

"I'll drink whisky too, please."

"And water?"

"Certainly."

"And water, please," said Davie to the porter. "Water is right. Do sit down."

"You'll be wondering who I am," said Donald.

"I've been wondering about that, off and on, all day."

"I'm the chauffeur," said Donald. "I'd have met you only—"

"Only I didn't say when I was coming."

"Yes. Lady Cassillis asked me to call on you—to tell you about everything—about the arrangements, I mean."

"Please tell me."

"The funeral's at eleven, at the church. Not here, of course."

"At West Tidwell?"

"Yes. There's a family vault."

"I remember."

In the silence that followed Davie went on remembering. He loved that fourteenth century church with its rood screen, the squint, and the carved pew-ends, and on the walls so many Cassillis memorials—particularly the one which took up far too much room in the little Lady Chapel, that of Sir Robert, 1690–1761, in full regalia, every curl of his vast wig carefully delineated in marble. He had been, so the inscription declared, a devoted husband, honoured by his children, beloved by his tenantry, pious, just, and beneficent. At his feet a woman crouched over a broken urn, but Sir Robert's gaze was turned heavenwards where a posse of rollicking cherubs eagerly directed him towards superior entertainments. It was clear that Sir Robert was in for a rousing reception if not a standing ovation.

Outside the porch there was a mighty yew tree. Beyond the churchyard wall lay an orchard, glorious in spring with apple blossom, daffodils and primroses.

"Afterwards Lady Cassillis hopes you will come to lunch," said Donald, breaking into Davie's memories. "And then, she says, if it suits you, you could look at the papers in the library in the afternoon."

"I'd like to do that."

The waiter brought the two glasses of whisky, an interruption which seemed to come as a relief to the young man. Donald was not an easy talker, and so far he had not told Davie anything that he wanted to know.

After some seconds Davie said, "Please tell me—how did it happen? I know nothing."

"Didn't Irene tell you?"

(Irene?)

"No."

"Robert died in his sleep. It was one of these coronaries. There's nothing to tell. Nothing at all."

But there was another question to be asked of this young man who called his employer by her Christian name, and Davie was not the person to deny his curiosity.

"So you are the chauffeur?" he said.

Donald Bride smiled a little sheepishly and looked down at the carpet.

"Yes. You are surprised. Well . . . Irene's father was my father's second cousin. She came across me in London when they came back from abroad. I was trying to write things. Struggling author. And she asked Robert if I could use the little house at the east lodge—they never use those gates—and keep myself by chauffeuring for them. Robert said yes. And that's what I've been doing."

"And have you managed to do both? It's difficult."

"If you don't plan it's difficult. But if you get up early enough—"

"Like Trollope. He wrote his books before breakfast."

"If you do that or something like it, it's all right," said Donald, rising from his chair. "Thank you for the drink. I think I ought to be off now. Tomorrow there will be a car for you from the garage. I ordered it for twenty to eleven."

"Thank you very much, and for coming."

Davie walked with him down the hotel steps and watched him climb into a low, red, open sports car. Then, instead of saying "Good night," he asked, "What do you write?"

"I'm struggling with a novel."

"Struggling is all right, and not to be despised. Only machines find that sort of thing easy."

"I have a consuming desire to make some money."

"That's all right too. Money is the root of all comfort. It was the *love* of money that St. Paul thought a bad thing. There has been a regrettable misunderstanding about that. Good night."

Donald Bride laughed, waved his hand, wheeled off to the left and shot up the High Street with a noise like a rocket. Following him into the street, Davie watched him disappear. Then turning sharp left himself, he walked up the short road beside the hotel to the cliff.

That was a strange young man, he was thinking. Not unattractive—but shy, was he? or nervous?

It was warm on the cliff with a slight air breathing from the west. The moon was up, striping the bay with silver. There was no other sound but the regular sound of waves breaking on the beach, and drawing the stones with them as they retreated. Advancing and retreating, advancing and retreating. It was a sound he had been brought up on. And, oh yes, he thought, old Matthew Arnold heard it at Dover, and Sophocles heard it on the Aegean, but neither of them heard it like this, not like this, not with these stones, not in the least like shingle.

Two miles away a bell tolled from the buoy on the sandbank. A melancholy sound that.

He turned to the right and started to walk up the steep cliff path. "These cliffs are dangerous," the notice board said. They always had been. He could see where paths he used to know had broken away and now lay smashed on the stones below.

Halfway towards the beacon the cliff top flattens out for a few hundred yards and at one place develops a deep cleft, where a little stream has for centuries been busy cutting its way towards the sea. The

Chine, as it was called, was a slippery declivity, between gorse and bramble and blackthorn, a way, but a dangerous way, down to the beach. Long ago a zigzag path had been cut in the sandstone, a little bridge laid across a gap and some steps cut at the bottom end of the descent. As a boy Davie had often come this way on bathing expeditions with Robert. But the path had fallen into disrepair long since; few used it now, though there still remained near the top a couple of well-hidden seats not unknown to the amorous young people of Tidwell St. Peter's. Davie went a little way down the path and sat on one of them. Everything about him was quite still. There was no sound but the sound of the sea, and that sad warning bell from the sandbank.

This had been a smuggler's path. He had remembered the Tidwell St. Peter's smugglers when Donald spoke of West Tidwell Church. Now he was thinking about them again. It was a memory that had always delighted him as a boy. Not so much as a hundred and fifty years ago Tidwell St. Peter's had been a famous smugglers' beach, and the favourite hiding place had been, under the vicar's protection, at the quiet church of West Tidwell. There are high oblong brick tombs in the churchyard that had held the kegs snugly, and under the personal direction of the good minister they had been stacked behind the battlements over the porch. The vicar—old Stapleton, he had been there fifty-eight years when he died— also accommodated a considerable store in a secret room built for the precise purpose in the vicarage walls. The house was still there, but nowadays it was The Old Vicarage, some later incumbent having removed himself, for some inscrutable reason, from a beautiful old house to an ugly Victorian one. Splendid old Stapleton! Alas, villainy at a distance sounds so romantic and exciting. But men got killed in those days, when the smugglers and the excisemen met each other. They carried the contraband from the beach up the cliff, sometimes from the cove further west, sometimes up this very path, and then it was taken across country to West Tidwell. Several gentlemen of Tidwell St. Peter's had been happy to lend their ponies for the expedition.

Villainy, Davie told himself again, is romantic at a distance. Villainy near to is villainy. We don't think lorry hijackers romantic. We are not endeared to the smuggler of Swiss watches, nabbed at the airport. Still—there were differences. The old smugglers had been local folk. Old Bill, and Jack, and the doctor and the vicar. They were against the law, and they had thought themselves justified. Damn it—it *had* been romantic.

It was late, nearly quarter to eleven, when he got back to the Ottery Arms. It had been a long day and he was quickly in bed. He did not feel like reading any of his books. So he put out the light and lay quite still listening to the sea, and thinking a little about Matthew Arnold, and Sophocles, and old Stapleton, and Robert, lying on the pebbles in the surf, with the waves advancing and retreating, advancing and retreating, and presently to that music he fell asleep, and did not stir until Rose called him at half past seven with his tea.

It was a bit strong and a bit overdrawn—as early morning tea often is in a hotel. Presumably it gets delayed in corridors, thought Dr. Davie, drowsily contemplating the clouds squared in his window frame.

They were moving, he was glad to see, at a proper pace. Not like those crazy projections they're so fond of in the theater nowadays.

More awake, he began to consider the day's trouble. Thank heaven the age of funeral pomp was past —the plumes, the crêpe, the black gloves and the widow's weeds. He could just remember some of that paraphernalia of mourning. And the black-edged writing paper—goodness, people had used that for months! It was all gone now, and a good thing too. But, for all that, he put on a dark suit and a black tie. He did not subscribe to the opposite idea either.

IV

When it was all over he had been thankful to escape upstairs into the peace of the library. Lunch had been terrible. Terrible to him, excruciating, he imagined, to Irene. There was Cousin Frances, who thought visible distress was proper to a funeral repast, and Cousin Grace, who considered that people's spirits should be kept up, and that she had been especially endowed by Providence for that purpose. There was Cousin George, who conducted his conversation in a hushed whisper, though whether for reasons of delicacy or laryngitis was not apparent, and Cousin Alfred, who, from pure embarrassment, laughed heartily at everything addressed to him. The only bearable relation, Davie thought, was Cousin Elinor. She said almost nothing to anyone but devoted herself with great single-mindedness to the pleasures of the table. "I am driving back to Chudleigh," she confided to Davie, "and I cannot do that without sustenance. The prawns are excellent."

As soon as he could gracefully do so Davie had gladly slipped upstairs to the long low room with its famous plaster ceiling and vast open fireplace. At first he could hear through the floor an occasional exhortation from Cousin Grace, or a nervous laugh from Cousin Alfred. But presently, when the visitors moved into the drawing room, the house grew quiet and Davie became totally involved in the pleasures of a library.

His true task was with the manuscripts. Most of these had been bound and stood neatly in order on the shelves. But on adjacent shelves there were books, and Davie kept taking them down with predictable consequences. There was Fanny Burney's diary, for instance, the early one. It was a long time since he had read that, and perched on the top of a flight of library steps, he was still reading it twenty minutes later when the sound of departing cars disturbed him. The cousins, praise be, were on the move. Davie replaced Fanny on the shelf and disciplined himself to duty. This was a first investigation to find what was there. He glanced through volumes of manuscript, peered into files, opened cupboards and drawers. Finally he sat down at Robert's great table to thumb through the loose papers which lay as he had left them.

Everything was mercifully tidy. There was not much in the table drawer. A variety of pencils. A ruler. A penknife. A small blue notebook. A book of stamps. Some writing paper. Envelopes.

Davie took out the notebook and turned over the pages. He had not meant to read it, but something caught his attention, and really, he thought, how odd, how very unexpected. He turned back to the beginning. There were only four pages of writing, but before he had finished reading them the door opened and Donald was standing there. "They've all gone, Dr. Davie," he said. "Thank God. It's five o'clock. Irene's had a rest, and there's tea in the drawing room, and she says, will you come."

"Indeed I will. Tea is an essential in my life. Especially today; I haven't been to sleep, and that's most unusual for me."

Slipping the notebook in his pocket, Dr. Davie followed Donald Bride down the stairs.

She was sitting on the sofa facing a wide fireplace. Great logs lay there waiting for winter, but now, in front of them, stood pots of hydrangeas. There is nothing gracefully frivolous about a hydrangea—those petals like pieces of paper. Compared to a columbine, the hydrangea seems more like an extension of the foliage than a flower. But it is a cool, collected, and dignified plant, and exactly right, so Davie thought, for Irene, who was all those things. She had exchanged her black frock for a mauvy-blue affair, which a dress catalogue might well have named "hydrangea." A little tired she looked, but she had a good colour, and she was ready to talk.

Donald sat in a deep chair on her left, Davie on her right in an upright wing armchair with claw and ball feet. "Not so far to go for my aged bones," said Davie. "It suits you," said Irene. "You look like an illustration to a Jane Austen novel."

Presently she asked, "Are things in pretty good order, R.V.?"

R.V. Robert had always called him that.

"Yes, indeed they are. There are a good many of these manuscript books. But they are tidy and plain. I don't think there will be any difficulty in preparing them for press. I take it that's what we're going to do. That's what you want."

"Yes, certainly I do."

"That's what I thought."

Davie set down his cup, drew the notebook out of his pocket, opened it, and turned the pages over without reading them.

Irene was busy pouring out tea for Donald.

"Tell me, Irene," Davie began, and hesitated.

"Yes? Tell you what?"

"Did Robert ever talk about writing a novel?"

"A novel? No—never."

"I found a notebook in a drawer, which reads like the first notes for a novel—a detective novel I would think."

"Detective novel? He never read them. I can't believe he'd have written one. What does it say?"

"It's just notes and not very clear. It seems to concern the death of one Adam Merrick, and—"

Davie checked and looked up from the page. Donald had moved suddenly in his chair.

"Does this strike a note?"

He was looking at Donald, but it was Irene who answered.

"Adam Merrick was a neighbour. He died last March."

"I see. Not fiction."

"No." She held out her hand. "Can I see?"

Davie leaned forward and handed her the notebook.

As she read he sat back in his chair and watched her over the top of his spectacles. She was a very beautiful woman, he was thinking. But so pale, so pale. Everything must have been a terrible shock to her. And the strain of entertaining all those ghastly cousins. . . .

For a minute no one spoke, and nothing moved in the room but Irene's fingers turning the few pages. When she had finished she handed the book back with a little sigh almost of relief.

"Adam Merrick had an accident," she said. "It was rather dramatic, but the police could find nothing wrong about it. You may be right. Perhaps the affair did give Robert an idea. He might have thought it was like the beginning of a detective novel, and was seeing what he could make of it."

"That wouldn't have been in the very best taste," said Davie after a long pause. "Perhaps he thought the police were mistaken and that there *was* something wrong with it. Perhaps he was trying his hand at sorting it out."

"Either way he didn't get very far. More tea, R.V.?"

It was evident that Irene had said all she meant to say about that.

Davie put the notebook back in his pocket. He said, "I have an inordinate craving for another piece of that cake." And so the conversation changed and presently he went up to the library again and stood by the shelves, taking down bound volumes of manuscript, turning their pages, putting them back again. The anthropological notes would require expert examination. They looked splendidly readable, but they

would need arranging. Perhaps Geoffrey Willow
would take it on. Willow was a Fellow at Davie's
Cambridge college, St. Nicholas's. The volumes of
autobiography were another matter. They looked
clean and ready. He would see that through the press
himself.

Crossing to the other side of the room, Davie paused
by the window. Unless you lived in that room, and
grew unconscious of its pleasures, it would be impossible not to pause by the window. It looked down
through diamond panes to a paved terrace, a border
of flowers, and a short flight of steps to another terrace of lawn. On the far side of the lawn was a low
stone wall pierced by another flight of steps which
led down to the rose garden. At the head of the steps
stood sentinel cypresses.

The rose garden was below Davie's line of sight. In
the distance, beyond the low wall, he could see the
rhododendrons and beyond them the shores of the
lake. Behind the lake, rising like a noble curtain,
were Cadleigh woods. It was the most peaceful and
the most romantic view that he had ever known. And
nowhere in the whole panorama was there a sign
of man.

Davie decided he had done enough for this day.
He wanted to walk down the terraces, at least to the
rose garden. He hoped it hadn't been altered. He
remembered it boxed in with hedges of yew, and, in
an apse at either end, the statue of a faun.

He left the library and went down the stairs. The
drawingroom door was open. He looked inside. There
was nobody there. The garden door was open. He
stepped out on to the terrace. There was nobody there

either. Nothing stirred but the bees in the flower beds. Behind a clump of magenta crane's-bill, Blanche, the white cat, lay exquisitely asleep.

He walked down the steps, crossed the lawn, and then went slowly down the next flight, between the cypresses, to the rose garden.

At the foot of the steps he paused and looked about him. The yew hedge stood immaculate: the fauns were still at their posts, a good deal patched with lichen, grey and yellow, but still the old memorials to naughtiness. Poor things, thought Davie, they hadn't seen much fun these thirty years—not during the tenancy of Miss Nora Cassillis, Robert's aunt, who had only departed this life two years before at the age of a hundred and six.

He did not think he would go down to the lake— it was too far and too late—but he crossed the rose garden to the arch in the yew hedge, the arch which made the entrance to the walk through the rhododendrons. And there he stood suddenly still.

Twenty-five yards away, their backs towards him, looking down towards the lake, Irene was standing beside Donald Bride. Her hand was lightly linked in his.

Quickly and quietly Davie walked back across the rose garden and up the two flights of steps to the house. It was already half past six. The car from Tidwell St. Peter's would be calling for him in a quarter of an hour. He decided to walk down the drive to meet it.

V

The Ottery Arms had begun as an early Victorian building. Over the years it had grown wings, and now the old house nestled incongruously between additions that were larger than itself. In one of these additions stood the bar. Davie was sorry that in smartening itself up it had become the cocktail bar, not that anyone ever drank cocktails there. Most people drank beer, the retired colonels drank whisky, the Navy gin, and a few ladies indulged in a mysterious mixture called port and lemon.

Davie always enjoyed that complex of doors which adorns the genuine old-fashioned pub: the saloon (or sometimes the private) door; the public door—the two bars divided from, and yet usually visible to, each other—and that other splendid door, the "Jug and Bottle Entrance." People may still use such a door to obtain bottles, but it isn't often, these days, that old ladies are seen tottering out of it carrying foaming jugs for private roistering at home. That seems a thing of the past—yet there the legend runs engraved on the glass doors of many ancient houses— Jug and Bottle Entrance—though not outside classy hotels, not outside a house like the Ottery Arms. Here people drink their beer in a cocktail bar, and the cocktail bar has lemon and pink geometrical shapes encrusted on the walls beneath dazzling lights, which, as everybody knows, is calculated to excite a suitably jovial attitude among the customers. Davie preferred the low ceiling and the rafters of a village

pub, or the plush and cut glass mirrors of the city.
But there it was, the drink was the same, and so, by
way of a change, at a quarter past seven, Davie went
down the corridor to the cocktail bar for his evening
support.

There were not many people there. In a far corner
a dull man and a dull woman were heads together
over a glass table and two glasses of stout. Two elderly men were talking bowls at one end of the bar.
At the other end was a short cheerful young man
with curly hair and freckles. Somewhere Davie had
seen him before, and somewhere the young man had
seen Davie before, for he came up to him at once
and said, "Good evening, Dr. Davie."

"Good evening. I know you very well by sight,"
said Davie, "but you must tell me who you are. I'm
bad at names."

"It's not really fair, because we haven't met. My
name's Giles Gifford and I'm an undergraduate—"

"At St. Nicholas's. I connected you at once with
something discreditable but I couldn't remember
what. Is this your home ground?"

"Almost. My father is vicar of West Tidwell."

"Then I think I saw him this morning. He was
taking the service at Sir Robert Cassillis's funeral."

"He was. Is that why you are here?"

"Yes. He was a very old friend. This is my home
ground too, in a sense. I used to live here when I
was a boy. It's odd coming back after many years.
It's not changed much."

"Are you staying long?"

"Some days. I've work to do at Cadleigh. I am the
literary executor."

"Ah," said Giles Gifford. After a pause he added, "I suppose you'll be looking into things."

"Literary things," said Davie. "Will you have a drink with me?"

A becoming pink mantled the cheek of young Mr. Gifford. He was not widely experienced in the etiquette of bar hospitality.

"Thank you very much."

"What shall it be?"

"A half of bitter, please."

"That's as modest a request as you can make in a bar. Have none of these noble bottles any message for you?"

"Not really. A half of bitter would be lovely."

"Very good. And a single whisky, please."

"Where did you live, Dr. Davie?"

Davie told him that, and so, very easily, they got talking about old Tidwell St. Peter's, and "Gosh!" said Giles Gifford, "it's like a book. Driving to picnics behind horses—in a brake—I wish I'd done that."

"Mind you, we didn't get far. Five miles to the castle—that was a long expedition."

"Yes—but I've never seen a brake, and never will."

"Well—we almost never saw a car, certainly didn't drive in one."

And then, as he perceived that Giles was working himself up to propose the other half, he said, "Twenty-five to eight. I think I must go to dinner. I'm glad we ran into each other."

"So am I. And thanks for the drink. And—and, Dr. Davie, if you want to know anything while you're here, do ask me. I know all the dope about everyone. If you should want any help I—well—my number's in the book. Gifford."

It was not immediately apparent how Giles's un-rivalled store of information about the citizens of Tidwell St. Peter's might be of service to Dr. R. V. Davie in his task as literary executor of Sir Robert Cassillis, but the offer seemed kindly meant, and so Davie said thank you, and good night, and retired down the corridor to the dining room.

And Giles Gifford looked at his watch and said "Help!" and set out for home in a very ancient car. He had told his mother he would be in for dinner, and he was late. But he had a splendid excuse—hob-nobbing with one of the dons of his college. His mother would be rather pleased, poor lamb.

Romantic youth that he was, as he drove through the lanes in the setting sun he couldn't help wonder-ing what old Davie was really up to.

VI

He was up to nothing at all. He was just staring at the white tablecloth between courses, and thinking about Irene. The sun aslant the roses, making long shadows on the lawn; and no sound in the rose gar-den, no sound at all, although, beyond the yew hedge, two people were standing, hand in hand, looking down towards the lake. Lady Cassillis and her chauf-feur, on the afternoon of the funeral—it sounded scandalous. But Irene and her cousin Donald, that was different. Davie found no blame, no questioning in his heart. It was natural that Irene should turn to Donald for support, and natural that he should give it.

Still, Davie was thankful they had not seen him. The explanation was obvious, but it would not have been possible to speak it.

Bertha brought the pudding. He had chosen junket and cream for old times' sake, and it was indeed the real thing. Clotted cream. Not to be got nowadays outside the west country, and not always there. (Though anyone could make it in London if he were prepared to buy enough raw material.) The real thing, and yet, like so many other things, not the same. In Davie's youth they had made it beside a wood fire or a peat fire, and you could taste it. Like the brake that Giles Gifford was destined never to ride in, people are never going to know how Devonshire cream tasted before the reign of the separator and the gas stove.

"Hail Progress!" thought Davie, and withdrew, but not dissatisfied.

Most of the diners had gone into the sun lounge. In the inner lounge there was only one woman in a corner, rattling on about her daughter to a patient friend, who interpolated little cries of agreement and commiseration from time to time but was otherwise put to no conversational strain.

". . . And then of course they turn to Grannie and want to know if I can have her, and I say no, dear, I can't. It's too much for me."

"Of course, dear, far too much."

"I told her how it would be . . ."

Davie collected a cup of coffee from the side table and sat down in the opposite corner. There he could hear only a background murmur except occasionally when the patient friend said "Oh *no!*" or "My *dear!*" It was far enough. He began to think of his plans.

He had to decide how long to stay. Fortunately it
was vacation time, but there were some engagements.
It might be necessary to go away and come down
again. He set down his coffee cup and put his hand
into his coat pocket to get his diary—and his fingers
closed on something unfamiliar. It was the blue notebook. It had not lived up to his hopes, that notebook, and he had forgotten about it. Now he took
it out and began to look at it again. And as he read
he saw between him and the page a picture of Irene
reading in the drawing room that afternoon; and he
remembered how pale she looked and her curious
little sigh of relief as she handed the book back. She
had not wished to talk about it. Which was under-
standable.

VII

ADAM MERRICK

The two woods are adjacent—only divided by the
lane that goes down to S's house on the outskirts of
the village.

The quarry is near the road, on the edge of the
wood, Merrick's wood. Disused, with a bit of water
in it most times of year. That's where he was found.
He'd fallen over the edge, hit his head on the way
down and drowned while unconscious.

Police can't find anything else. If he fell over that
would account.

It was his own land so they don't have to ask why
he was there.

But he was on his way back from S when it happened. There's evidence about that. And path goes

near the edge of the quarry. It isn't properly railed. When he got there he must have left the path. Trespassers or poachers.

Mrs. M called in their neighbour Jason. G.G. helped. They found him together. The police have not taken it up. It does seem watertight.

The writing had been on four right-hand pages of the notebook, and it had covered only a small part of the fourth page. The exposition had come to a plain end, and neither Irene nor Davie had turned that last page over. He did so now.

There was nothing on the right-hand page, but on the top of the left page there was one further word—"Irene." That was all—and Robert had scratched it out.

Well . . . the notes were exciting, but their purpose was not apparent. According to the police there *was* no mystery. So why the worry?

He put the notebook back in his pocket and very gladly picked up a book in a bright yellow jacket, fruitfully titled *Dead Man's Evidence*.

There was a mystery there all right.

VIII

The front door was open when he arrived next morning. The hall was full of flowers. But there was no sound of Irene or anyone else. Davie peeped into the drawing room. There was no one there. So he went up the great stairs to the library.

On Robert's table there was a bowl of roses. Irene. And a note addressed to Davie.

> Dear R.V., I am sorry I missed you last night. I had gone down to the lake. Today I have to go to Exeter. Solicitors. Please do just what you want. Barnes will give you luncheon. Irene.

So he had had an uninterrupted morning on Robert's papers. It was easy work. So far as the papers were concerned, he could go home tomorrow. But there was a thought stirring in Dr. Davie's head as he went down to the rose garden after luncheon. He was not sure that he wanted to go home. Last night he had put the thing away from him—but that was partly because he wanted to finish *Dead Man's Evidence* (which incidentally had been a cheat, because Annabel Champion had basely concealed the fact that Miss Murchiston had made enquiries at the lunatic asylum, which was not fair). Last night he had put the thought from him, but he realized now that it had refused to go. He sat down on a teak bench, the yew hedge rising majestically behind him, cast a conspiratorial glance around the rose beds, and drew the blue notebook from his pocket once again.

They were strange notes, but surely he ought to be able to construe them. Was Robert reviewing the facts because he thought there might be something the authorities had missed? If so, as Irene had remarked, he had not got very far.

Or was he reviewing the facts because he knew they *did* contain something dangerous? "It does seem watertight." It was almost as though he were saying "It's O.K." It did not sound like Robert.

He turned the page. "Irene," crossed out. What was Robert going to write about Irene? And had the name any connection with the speculation on the earlier pages? There was no guessing that. And why do I keep on seeing her so pale, said Davie to himself. It isn't true. She has been bright as a daisy. She wasn't pale at that ghastly lunch party. She wasn't pale when we came down to tea yesterday. It was only when she was reading the notebook that she looked so white. It was my fault. I didn't know it was a true story, but it was consummately tactless of me to bring up a thing like that on that particular day.

For several minutes Dr. Davie sat on, staring at the roses. Then he got up and strolled along the paved walk and looked at the faun in the eastern apse of the yew hedge. Then he went down the other path and stared at the faun in the western apse. Yesterday he had reflected that the fauns hadn't seen any fun for thirty years. Perhaps he was wrong.

"It does seem watertight." He might find some other explanation of Robert's notes if only he knew a bit more about Adam Merrick. If only he knew a little more about it all.

He was still thinking the same thoughts two hours later as he sat in the sun lounge at the Ottery Arms, drinking tea. It was interesting, certainly it was. There was an air of mystery about it, and it was a case that the police had not taken up. On previous occasions he had felt embarrassed, circling around the edge of a problem which was officially being investigated by somebody else. But here there were no competitors. For the first time he would not be interfering. Of course the police might be right. Probably there *was* no problem. But it was interesting. And then Dr. Davie smacked his knee and said out loud "Of course," greatly to the surprise of an old lady, who stirred in her basket chair and looked nervously at him over the top of her spectacles. There was nobody else in the sun lounge. If he did it again . . . but Dr. Davie did not do it again. He got up and went down the passage to the telephones, where, after a brief examination of the directory, he dialled a number and asked for Mr. Giles Gifford.

"Speaking," said Giles Gifford. "You're Dr. Davie."

"How did you guess?"

"I thought you'd ring up sooner or later," said Giles. "You want some information."

It was a statement rather than an enquiry.

"Well, yes," said Davie. "I did want to ask you some questions."

"O.K.," said Giles. "How would it be if you went for a walk along the West Tidwell Road, and I met you in my car?"

"That would be very kind."

"If we go for a short drive we can talk without being under observation—in so far as it's possible to do anything without observation in this old-world resort. Would that suit you?"

"Admirably."

"Now? Right away?"

"Why not?"

"See you, then," said Giles. "In about ten minutes."

The telephone clicked in his ear, and Davie, marvelling a little, went into the cloakroom and supplied himself with a hat.

Then he set off along the West Tidwell Road.

TWO

I

"Where are you taking me?" asked Davie.

"To the top of the hill," said Giles Gifford.
"There's a gate with a view."

"I know it well."

"We can draw in there and have a look. And then
you can ask me questions."

"What made you so sure that I would want to ask
questions?"

"You have a reputation, sir, for sleuthing."

"Oh, nonsense!"

"And as soon as I saw you I guessed you were en-
quiring about that business last March."

"Which business?"

Giles gave him a sidelong look.

"The Merrick business."

"I didn't know anything about it till yesterday."

"I dare say. But now you do. And now you're asking. You see, Dr. Davie, I've been all through this
too, and I've never felt satisfied either. Did you know
I found him? I and Mr. Jason."

Of course, thought Davie, Robert's notes. Something about Jason. "G.G. helped. They found him
together." But he said nothing.

Giles had turned off the West Tidwell Road and

was driving uphill between high sandstone banks. Young oaks stretched their arms across the road like a vaulted roof. Then, suddenly emerging into the open, he brought the car to a stand beside a gap in the hedge and a five-barred gate.

Davie and Giles got out and stood there side by side. From here everything to the south and east and north lay open beneath them—the fields, the water meadows, the river valley, and, beyond the river, fields again, rising to cliffs above the neighbouring bay. Away to the right was Tidwell St. Peter's and the sea.

"I thought you'd like to see this," said Giles.

"Every particle in that prospect has altered since I saw it last," said Davie, "but the effect is precisely the same. I could swear there was always a foxglove at exactly that place in the hedge."

"And always a small boat at precisely that ripple in the bay, and the same number of gulls trespassing on the fields."

"On the other hand," said Davie, "I do see some black and white cows. They ought to be red-brown. I don't think I approve of that."

Old Dr. Davie and young Mr. Gifford leant together on the gate and stared at the river valley with deep satisfaction.

"It's a pity about the church," said Davie, pointing up the valley towards a village in a mist of trees. "One of Lady Ottery's nineteenth century outrages. The old gorgon pulled down a fourteenth century church and put up that wholly improbable granite affair to the greater glory of Lady Ottery. I believe she also removed a neolithic circle from the moor to make a rockery in her garden."

This, as young Mr. Gifford understood, was skirmishing. He waited a few seconds. Then he said:

"Come on, Dr. Davie, tell me what you want to know."

"I want to know the whole thing," said Davie, gazing fixedly towards the water meadows. "Who was this Adam Merrick? And why did his death, which passed for accident with the police and the coroner, arouse an uneasiness in my friend Robert Cassillis?"

"It did, did it?"

"I think so. And why does it arouse uneasiness in you?"

"There isn't a great deal to tell," said Giles Gifford. "But what there is is entirely unpleasant. At least, so it seems to me."

II

"First I must explain about Ernest Stubbings," said Giles. "This place is full of people honourably retired from running the world, and without the smallest future intention of running anything more exhausting than the bridge club—which is, of course, pretty exhausting. The place is administered by a few amiable people with a stake in the town's prosperity, and they do it very well. About six years ago this Ernest Stubbings came to live in Tidwell St. Peter's, but, unlike the other nabobs, he came to the place with the dedicated intention of running it. He had a mania for power, I suppose. He'd have run anything, but he happened to find Tidwell St. Peter's and decided he'd run that. He took a house called Quarry View, because it looks across the brook to the quarry—"

"*The* quarry?" asked Davie. "The one where Merrick was found?"

"Yes. But that wasn't grand enough for Stubbings. He altered the name to Gonville Lodge."

"Ha!"

"And he hadn't been there six months before he'd got out an election address in which he offered unselfish service to the people of Tidwell St. Peter's, and undertook, if I remember rightly, to represent everybody's interests without fear or favour."

"Difficult," murmured Davie.

"Yes, but the proposition appeared so fortunate to the electors that they returned the said Stubbings at the top of the poll. Nobody knew anything about him, but he was prepared to do the job, and that was enough for them. They were grateful. Within six months he had been elected to the chair by his equally grateful fellow councillors, and there he remained for three glorious years until Adam Merrick came along and took Pinewood, the house in the trees. The property goes as far as the top of the quarry. On the south side it slopes down to the brook, which on the other side is the boundary of several Tidwell St. Peter's gardens, including Ernest Stubbings's."

"Ah," said Davie, "neighbours and boundaries. Go on."

"Gonville Lodge—I'll show it to you presently—is a lamentable affair with red bricks and yellow bricks arranged in a pattern and a slate roof. Of course nobody architected it. It was run up by a builder before the days of planning. But it had an orchard that sloped down to the brook. It would have been pretty if the insufferable Stubbings had kept it as it was. But that wasn't what he wanted. The autumn after Merrick came, Stubbings cut down the trees and covered the slope with flower beds. You can see them a mile off because everything has to be arranged in a pattern: an oblong of white, an oblong of blue, an oblong of orange, all fitting together like a Chinese box, and pink in the center. Alyssum, lobelia, marigold, geranium. It's like a sweet shop. And that's what Adam Merrick found himself looking at when his first spring came round."

"He was against flower beds."

"He was, but the real trouble was the brook. Merrick planted a mass of daffodils on his side. Stubbings put up a lot of damned silly miniature windmills and some plaster storks which were bigger than the windmills. That infuriated Merrick, but there was nothing he could do about it. And then last March Stubbings decided to make a water garden, and to do that—"

"I know what you're going to say: he diverted the stream."

"Exactly."

"Cursed is he that removeth his neighbour's landmark."

"Amen. 'Cursed,' I understand, was the word. Merrick had been away for a week. In the early evening when he went down to look at his daffodils, then in their top glory, he found the brook a mass of mud, with a dam built across it and a whole lot of canals cut in the opposite bank between fatuous little islands, and Stubbings's man busy erecting miniature

Japanese bridges and pagodas all over the place. I suppose the channel must have filled up again in time. But the hazel-fringed, forget-me-not brook was gone."

"This was last March?"

"March thirteenth. It was the day that Adam Merrick died."

III

At half past five on that day in March, the day that Adam Merrick died, Rachel Merrick had been standing at her drawing-room window, looking down through the pine trees to the bay.

"He isn't faithful to me. Why should I be faithful to *him*?"

She spoke quietly, but the effect was calculated. Rachel Merrick had a great sense of drama, and about as much humour as the heroine of a Verdi opera.

The man who was standing behind her with his hands on her shoulders laughed softly.

"No reason at all, sweetheart," he said. "And, as you know very well, you are not."

"Basil, whose side are you on?"

"Yours, darling, but you mustn't invent your own rules in this game. It confuses the other players."

"All right, but what are we to do?"

"I've told you. Break away."

"And I've told *you*. You haven't enough money."

"Is it all that important?"

"Don't be childish. I can't do without money."

"And Adam has it."

"I'm never sure what from—but yes, Adam has it."

"And so Adam wins."

"So it seems. I don't know why he always should. There must be a way."

Rachel Merrick turned from the window, crossed the room, and stood for a few seconds beside a bowl of mauve tulips on a round marquetry table. So closely she resembled the leading lady in a drawing-room comedy, the action might have been carefully rehearsed. Then she moved on and sat down by the open hearth. The light was beginning to fade in the room. To Basil Jason by the window one side of her face was in shadow, the other bright in the glow of the log fire.

Ranged round the edge of the wide hearthstone were several lumps of rough-hewn coloured stone, black, white, green, purple, and flaming orange, chunks of material torn from the side of the world. Rachel Merrick had brought them back from the Mediterranean two summers before.

Basil Jason looked out of the window again at the March afternoon: daffodils in the grass, rhododendrons in bud, and the sun sloping down behind the pine trees. Adam's garden, he was thinking, and Rachel's room. He did not like Adam Merrick. He was besotted with Adam Merrick's wife and accepted her prejudices without question. To Basil Jason, Rachel's beauty was as glittering as the coloured stones at her feet. Entrapped in which simile, anyone not blinded by love might have added, "and as hard."

"There must be a way," said Rachel Merrick. "I'm tired of living with someone I hate." And as she spoke she looked across the room at Basil Jason, and he looked across the room at her. It was as though they agreed on some unspoken contract, he in the fading light of a March afternoon, she crouched by the fire.

It was dramatic, and meant to be dramatic, but specialist as she was in the tense situation, Rachel Merrick had not known the delicacy of her own timing. In the silence that followed that exchange of minds, wheels crunched on the gravel outside, and gaily a horn sounded three loud honks. The master of Pinewood had returned.

"Adam," said Rachel, getting up. She crossed the room, put on the light, stood a moment before a long glass, patting her hair into shape.

Then she opened the drawing-room door, and as she did so the front door opened.

"Hallo!" said Adam Merrick, plonking down a bag on the tiled floor.

"Darling!" said Rachel. "You're *much* earlier than I expected."

"I know. You'll think me absurd—but I wanted to get a sight of the daffodils by the brook before the light goes. So I hurried."

"I'm sure they're eagerly waiting for you," said Mrs. Merrick coldly, adding in another kind of voice, "Basil's here."

"Hullo, Basil," said Adam, without enthusiasm.

"We've had tea. Do you want anything?"

"No, thanks. I'll be back for a drink."

The front door banged. Rachel Merrick returned to the drawing room.

"You see."

"Yes, I do."

Standing by the window, she watched her husband walking downhill through the pine trees.

"Always those damned daffodils. He'll go down to the brook, oh yes—but it's only three minutes there and three minutes back. I don't expect to see him for an hour. He'll go on up to the wood. He meets someone there. I'm certain he does."

"Why should you care?"

"Because I don't like to be neglected, even if I do want to be free of him."

"If what you say is true, doesn't that give you the chance you need?"

"I hate all the shaming business of detection."

"That wasn't entirely what I meant," said Jason.

Rachel Merrick looked at him through half-closed eyes until he looked away. She liked to make him do that.

"The chance *you* need," she said.

Basil Jason shuffled awkwardly on his feet and turned aside. "I must be going," he said. "I've got things to do."

"You change the subject," said Rachel, moving back to the fire.

"See you tomorrow."

"I expect so."

Mrs. Merrick waited for the sound of the front door. Then she got up, crossed the room and put out the light. For a moment she stood before the long glass, enchanted with what she saw there in the red glow of the fire. Then she went into the hall, slipped on a coat and tied a silk scarf round her head. Adam must have left the brook long ago. Unless he had gone for a walk along the road, he must have gone up to the pinewood above the quarry.

It was growing dark, but she would be able to see her way, and presently the moon would be rising.

She put the big electric torch in her coat pocket. It would be darker in the wood. But first she took the path through the pines towards the daffodils.

IV

Giles Gifford could not tell Davie precisely that story. But he did know a great deal. He knew the blunt outline of the affair between Rachel Merrick and Basil Jason, the Merricks's next-door neighbour. That was no secret to the wide-eyed denizens of Tidwell St. Peter's.

"What does this Basil Jason do?" asked Davie.

"I believe he travels round selling expensive things on commission—like bottles of scent at £10 a go. I don't know where he gets it from—probably brews it in the back kitchen. He's also on the local council —a dumb supporter of the intolerable Stubbings. It doesn't occupy much of his time. The rest is dedicated to Mrs. Merrick. They go for walks," said Giles with a faint smile and a wicked emphasis on the word "walks."

And Giles had heard old Challice give his stolid account of what happened at the brook.

"He come down to the brook, Mr. Merrick did," Challice would say to anyone who was prepared to listen, "and he hollered out to me, what the blazes are you doing there, Challice, and I says to him, I'm making these yer little islands for Mr. Stubbings, I says. You've diverted the brook, he says, and you've no right to do it. Well, I says, you must go and tell that to Mr. Stubbings, I says, and I will that, he says, and off he goes out of his back gate and up to Quarry View, as it used to be called. It were getting dark then, so I went up to the shed and put my things away, and all the time I could yer Mr. Merrick shouting away at Mr. Stubbings and Mr. Stubbings shouting back at Mr. Merrick. It were a proper old caper."

And there the old man would stop, grieved that his story was done. It had been time for his tea, and nothing had seemed important enough to delay that ceremony. So, "Ah, it were a proper old caper," he would repeat, and shake his head as though he could tell more if he would.

But Giles also knew something of what had passed between Merrick and Stubbings from one Arthur Parsley, who lived on his own in Rose Cottage, which stood cheek by jowl with Gonville Lodge. He had heard from him how Merrick had raged out into the night, and how Stubbings had followed him to his gate, and even beyond—at least Arthur Parsley thought so. Ernest Stubbings denied this. Well, *someone* had followed Merrick down the lane. Arthur Parsley felt sure about that.

Giles had been having a drink at Basil's that night. He had been asked for half past six, but Basil had not come in till a quarter to seven and had looked surprised to see him, which was embarrassing. The whole entertainment had been rather sticky. And then Mrs. Merrick had burst into the house at about half past seven, calling "Basil! Adam's not come back. I'm sure something—" And then she had seen Giles and hesitated, but Giles had said, "Can I do anything, Mrs. Merrick?" and Rachel Merrick, after considering a moment, had said, "Yes, Giles, you can.

I wish you'd help Basil look for Adam. He's been gone more than two hours, and he said he'd be back soon."

Giles looked at Davie. It was a good place in the story to pause.

"You haven't told me just who Adam Merrick was," said Davie.

"He was rather a mystery. He used to take people for cruises in the Mediterranean in a yacht called *Rachel,* after his wife. He kept her at Salcombe, I believe. It must have paid well. He had lots of boodle."

"Ah," said Davie, detaching himself from the five-barred gate. It was time to move.

"Would you like to see the quarry?" said Giles.

"Yes, please, I would; though I know it well enough. It was there when I was a boy. We used to play rather frightening games in it. Who owns it?"

"I'm not sure; Mrs. Merrick, I suppose. Merrick's property, what *was* Merrick's property, starts immediately from the top of it. I think the council has some rights in the quarry. Occasionally a cart dumps rubbish in the corner among the nettles. It's probably private, but anyone can walk into it, and there won't be anyone there to raise the matter. We'll go down the hill and hairpin back on the next lane to the left. That returns to the village between Cadleigh woods and Merrick's woods."

"I know exactly."

Two minutes later Giles drew up at the side of the road. "I won't drive right up to it," he said. "Better to walk round the bend of the road. It won't attract notice. Do you agree?"

"Certainly."

"There it is," said Giles, when they had turned the corner, "and there, beyond the brook, you won't need to be told what that is."

He pointed to an emetic blaze of flower beds incised on the suffering grass and looking like the flag of some international organization.

"The stately pleasure gardens of Mr. Stubbings, I presume."

"Precisely."

"How truly appalling!"

At the unbarred entrance to the quarry Davie halted. "It *is* private," he said, pointing to a rickety notice board which peered at them from the branches of an elder bush.

"So it is," said Giles. "Come on in."

The sandstone quarry had not been used for years, and it had put on that strange beauty that the works of man assume while in the process of returning to nature. In the foreground great bramble bushes had covered much of the floor. Further in were several young trees, a sycamore, and two or three oaks bred from the casual acorn. There was so much greenery that a trespasser might be almost entirely screened from the road.

In a corner to the left was a shed, solid-looking but half surrounded with nettles and willow-herb. A gorse bush stood before the padlocked door.

The quarry was totally quiet, utterly deserted, and yet not without evidence of the occasional visitor—a broken edge of turf, a low branch of bramble crushed by a foot, a sodden matchbox lost in the bracken.

At the back, tall and sheer, the red sandstone face of the quarry glowed in the sunset.

The right half of the quarry was the part that

held water and made a pond in winter time. It was nearly dry now.

Giles took Davie to that place.

"This was where he was lying. Face down in the water. Of course there was a lot more water here in March. The inquest found that he had hit his head in falling and drowned while concussed."

Davie looked up to the rim of the quarry. It was far enough to fall. "Hit his head against what?" he said. "There's nothing on the way down."

"Something hard on arrival."

"He was face down in the water?"

"Yes, he was."

"And there aren't any rocks."

"No, but the police did remove a boulder. The theory was that he hit his head against that."

"Ah."

"I'll give you the newspaper report."

The shallow pool was full of those strange expected things which people love to dump in old quarries. A twisted bicycle wheel, the hood of a pram, a single boot, the spokes of an umbrella. And all those broken things had a history beginning with dignity. As much a history, thought Davie, as a man's broken body lying beside them in the same murky water.

"Was he damaged at all except for the head?"

"No, I don't think so. It's high over there in the center of the circle. Not so high here at the end of the crescent. The water would have broken his fall. If it hadn't been for the rock perhaps he'd have been all right."

"You began by saying you weren't satisfied. Now you're producing possible explanations. What didn't you like about it, eh?"

"I didn't like his being there at all. Why should he go peering over the top of the quarry? And why should he fall if he did?"

"You mean, I suppose, the old question—did he fall or was he pushed?"

"Well, something like that, Dr. Davie, yes."

"Let's go up above."

It meant skirting some brambles and pushing through bracken, but that was not difficult. It was no distance.

Once Davie stubbed his toe on a large stone and was neatly fielded by Giles.

"Steady, sir!"

"Thank you," said Davie. "Damn and blast them! Stones have no right in bracken."

Half a minute later he was looking over the edge of the quarry. At this point it was not more than a thirty-foot drop.

"This is the place?"

"Yes."

"Immediately above where you found him?"

"Yes."

Looking straight down, Davie examined the ruined pond. The bicycle wheel, the pram hood and the boot were some way to the right. Immediately below him he could see the spokes of the umbrella.

He looked about him. Perhaps last March the short turf had been disturbed. It was not disturbed now. He lay down flat and peered at the face of the quarry. Here certainly there were signs of dislodgement, but so there were all round the quarry. The soft red sandstone is perpetually eroded.

Why would anyone want to come here? Why leave the path on a dark evening to peer over the edge of a quarry—and at what? If he fell there was nothing mysterious about his being killed. But why had he been there at all? Giles was right there.

Davie pulled himself back on his knees and straightened himself up. As he did so he looked across the left half of the gravel pit, to the field beyond, to the little brook, to Mr. Stubbings's water garden; and like a wink of semaphore the last of the sun flashed back at him from the shadow of a laurestinus.

"I think perhaps we had better go," he said to Giles. "Don't stare across at Mr. Stubbings's garden. In a manner of speaking we are not alone. Mr. Stubbings, or I presume it to be Mr. Stubbings, is giving us his close attention."

"I was afraid that might happen," said Giles. "Come on. If we take the path we can walk round behind the quarry. It comes out near where we parked the car."

They pushed through the bracken and reached a narrow path through the pine trees.

"Any ideas, Dr. Davie?"

"None, except that Mr. Stubbings is interested in us."

"Stubbings is interested in everything. He is the aboriginal prodnose."

Silently, Indian file, they moved along the path, their feet making no sound on the carpet of pine needles. Between the dark pillars of the trees the western sky hung down in strips of rose and apricot. The glorious effect, Davie noted, was precisely the one that he resented when he saw it not inaccurately depicted on a calendar. Were they too easy to represent, all those forest clearings, Scottish or Canadian, trees in the sunset, trees in the snow? The thoughts of Dr. R. V. Davie roved with peculiar agility. A moment later he was far away, contemplating with repugnance a picture of an Australian gum tree caught in the pink light of dawn.

He was brought back to the moment by Giles laying a sudden hand on his sleeve.

A hundred yards ahead they could see where the path joined the road. From the same gap in the hedge another path led through the pine trees at right angles to the one they were on. A man and woman were walking along it. To Davie's eyes they were silhouettes, but Giles knew who they were.

"Mrs. Merrick and Basil Jason," he said in a low voice. "And that's Basil's house over there."

"How interesting!" said Davie. "Everyone in this story lives near the old quarry. Are they engaged?"

"Not announced."

"What is known as 'just good friends' perhaps?"

"They ought to be," said Giles. "For a long time they've been as thick as—"

" 'Thieves' is the accepted comparison," said Davie.

"I was thinking of something more like Clytemnestra and Aegistheus."

"Oh, were you, indeed?" said Davie. "In that case I think you'd better keep your thoughts to yourself."

By the gap in the hedge, where the two paths joined the road, there were gorse bushes sprinkled with gold.

"When the gorse is out of bloom, kissing's out of fashion," quoted Davie. "It's true. Somehow—one kind or another—it never is."

"I was only thinking about who benefitted," said Giles, opening the car door.

"How do you know who benefitted?" said Davie.
"Those perhaps are two. There may be others."

Giles, a little rebuked, drove him back to the Ottery Arms.

V

Giles had got it on his innocent mind that he ought
to return Davie's hospitality, and so on reaching the
hotel he said, "Dr. Davie, will *you* have a drink with
me this evening?" And, because Davie knew that it
would please Giles if he said yes, he said yes, he
certainly would and allowed himself to be conducted
to the bar.

"I remember what yours is," said Giles.

"Alas! How embarrassing to be identified with a
bottle. But yes, please, at this time of day that would
be precisely right."

So Davie settled down at a little table in a corner,
and sat back to enjoy the pageant of Tidwell society,
and presently Giles joined him with the drinks.

"We're in luck," he said. "The mighty Stubbings
has just come in."

"Which one?"

"The pompous little man with the beady eyes and
the bald dome. I bet you he'll come over and speak."

The bar at the Ottery Arms is not large, and bar
conversations are not usually of a confidential character. No one particularly minds being overheard.
The difference between Ernest Stubbings and any
other patron of the Ottery was the fact that he con-

ducted his conversation with the manifest intention of being overheard, and indeed would frequently look about him as he spoke, to satisfy himself that the record of his achievements (for Mr. Stubbings spoke of nothing else) was being clearly received by the company. Anyone conversing with Mr. Stubbings was in the position of a feed. Mr. Stubbings's observations were not addressed to his apparent audience.

"And so I said to him"—his voice rang strongly above the laughter and talk—"you are not only wrong in fact, my friend, you are wrong in principle. He never said another word. Not another word. He just turned round and slunk off. He knew me, and he knew I meant what I said."

Without wiping off the fat, triumphant smile which had illustrated his story, Mr. Stubbings cast a quick glance round the room, sniffed, gave a little shake of his head and returned to Mr. Smallpiece, Mr. Stubbings's principal yes man on the parish council.

"You had him there," said Mr. Smallpiece.

"Evening, Blizzard," said Mr. Stubbings, suddenly transferring his patronage to a more valuable acquaintance. Blizzard was the senior partner in Blizzard and Harbottle, estate agents. "Evening, Blizzard. I was hoping I'd see you. How are you fixed tomorrow? I'd like to have a few minutes with your good self—"

"Dear God!" murmured Davie. "Not that—"

"Steel yourself," said Giles. "Stubbings is about to have an accidental word with me on his way out." And indeed a minute later Mr. Stubbings raised his eyebrows in apparent surprise and stopped beside their table.

"Well, young Gifford," he said, with a ghastly smile confidently intended to purvey a flavour of waggishness, "what have you been up to, eh?"

"Up to?" said Giles.

"Yes, up to. You didn't see *me* this afternoon, but I saw *you*. What were you doing on top of the quarry, eh? Dangerous place up there. It ought to be railed."

"I was looking for butterflies, if you must know," said Giles.

"Butterflies?"

"Yes, there's a special kind we get down here which likes the gorse—"

"Oh," said Mr. Stubbings, taking a long look at Davie, who was staring with great concentration into the bottom of his glass. "Well—mind you're careful, my lad."

"I will be that," said Giles. "Good night."

Mr. Stubbings had not actually been in motion when Giles said good night, but then finding it difficult to stay, he raised a pudgy hand and said, "Good night, Gifford."

Davie and Giles watched the glass door close behind him. "I didn't introduce you on purpose," said Giles.

"So I observed," said Davie. "With admiration."

"That man's curiosity is boundless. He wants to run everything. He *does* run everything. He's hand in glove with Blizzard the estate agent, and he's got a partnership with Walter Ford, who's king of the lobster pots and looks like a pirate. Probably is one. Stubbings contributes a motorboat, and Walter contributes lobsters. At least that's what we're given to understand."

"Sounds a bit unequal to me," said Davie. "Well, thank you for my drink. And now I think I ought to move on. It's dinner time."

"You must stay a minute, Dr. Davie. Here's another bit of luck. Arthur Parsley. You've got to meet Arthur. Tell me—do you know anything about snowstorms? Those glass things you shake."

"Yes," said Davie.

"I thought you would," said Giles, waving a hand at a man who was just collecting his drink at the bar. "Hi, Arthur! Come over here!"

"Hullo, Giles," said the man, steering in their direction. He was tall, bronzed, blue-eyed, admirably dressed in a biscuit-coloured linen suit. His deep blue shirt was open at the neck. He was, Davie guessed, forty and every elegant inch a bachelor.

"Arthur, I want you to meet a friend of mine," said Giles, "Dr. Davie. He knows all about snowstorms. Will you be an angel and show him your collection?"

"Yes, of course. How d'you do?"

"How d'you do? That's very kind of you. I needn't say that I *don't* know all about snowstorms, but I do adore them. One doesn't see as many of them as one used to see—I suppose because they were essentially cottage ornaments. Perhaps people got rid of them when they started living in horrid little villas with healthy lino on the floor and suites of damnably uncomfortable furniture. A snowstorm wouldn't have looked sufficiently up to date. What do you think?"

"I live in a genuine thatched cottage," said Arthur, "with roses all over it. Moreover, it's called Rose Cottage."

"I'm so glad," said Davie. "Well done."

"The ceilings are low, and there are beams all over the place. It's extremely difficult to get up the stairs, the bedroom floors are cock-eyed, and the windows have diamond panes. In *my* cottage there are lots of snowstorms. When will you come to see them?"

"Thank you, I'll be delighted. Can it be tomorrow? I'm going back to London the day after."

"Tomorrow will be fine. Would six o'clock be a good time?"

"Eminently."

"Will you come, Giles?"

"Thanks very much."

"I shall look forward to this," said Davie. "But now, Giles, I really must go, or I shall miss—God knows what I may miss."

"Don't delay a moment," said Arthur Parsley.

"See you tomorrow at Rose Cottage," said Davie.

VI

After dinner Davie walked slowly down the hotel steps, crossed the courtyard and turned into the High Street. There was no one about. Full of thought, he walked with downcast eyes, his hands folded together like a monk, not looking at all in the shop windows, as was his habit. Beguiled partly by Robert's note-book and partly by the imagination of a romantic young man, he had been induced to take an interest in a mystery which might, he supposed, evolve into something dangerous, or might, he expected, subside into a mare's nest. He had allowed himself to peer about, looking for evidence. And what had he collected? Nothing at all. Only a few facts.

Adam Merrick and Ernest Stubbings had quarrelled.

Mrs. Merrick and Basil Jason were lovers.

Adam Merrick had taken people for cruises in the Mediterranean.

Irene had seemed vaguely disturbed by the discovery of Robert's notebook. She had seemed relieved after reading it.

Donald had stirred at the unexpected mention of Adam's name.

Donald and Irene were close friends—whether more than close friends he did not know, and would not guess.

That was all—except, yes, except that Basil Jason had been late for his drinks party. A wispy little fact, but anything could be important. Davie stored it away in his mind.

As for the facts at the quarry—it was hardly surprising that, last March, there had seemed to be no case for the police. A man had fallen over a precipice and killed himself. It has happened before. They had not found anything that involved anyone else.

Nevertheless one thought returned to his mind relentlessly, and must have returned to anybody's mind who ever thought about it. If Adam Merrick fell over the edge of the quarry, he must have approached it. And why the devil should he do that? Why at any time, least of all, why in the dark, when there would be nothing to see? Or could there have been something to see? Something illuminated. In the quarry? It seemed widely improbable.

Davie left the High Street behind him and walked

on in the direction of Exeter between houses and gardens he remembered from childhood, and presently he turned down a road to the right. So far he had avoided this road. Houses he had loved and lost he never could bear to see again. But this evening he walked on, and when, presently, the road curved slightly to the left, there it was. The house looked entirely unchanged, but the garden—the garden where the infant Davie had dug for pennies planted by his father, the garden where the doctor had kindly called to visit one of the rabbits alleged by the children to be poorly (doctors have no time these days for such gentle acts)—the garden was different. The shrubbery was down. The pear tree was down. And, worst of all, the great oak tree was down. The *oak tree*—how could they?

He ought not to have come, he told himself as he turned about and made his way back to the village.

But now he was more like himself again—inquisitive. Cheeses and stationery, ironmongery and Anna Marie, Ladies' Fashions—they were all the same to Dr. R. V. Davie. He loved shop windows and he looked at the lot, including those of Blizzard and Harbottle, house agents. Desiring nothing, he nevertheless gave his attention to the desirable residences so warmly recommended to the public, and there, between No. 20 Ottery Terrace, and Restawhile (the owner evidently having rested long enough) was a card that reawakened his interest in Giles Gifford's mystery. Pinewood was to be let furnished for the winter months. To be seen by appointment only.

Standing there on the pavement, Dr. Davie made an immediate decision. He would call upon Blizzard and Harbottle first thing tomorrow morning. He very much wanted to inspect Mrs. Merrick's desirable residence. With any luck he might have an opportunity of inspecting Mrs. Merrick.

That settled, he ambled on down the High Street, pausing a moment to remember old Mrs. Veitch and the lemonade bottles, peering in at the windows of two antique shops (goodness, what prices!), and so returned to the Ottery Arms.

Before going to bed he telephoned to Irene and told her he would come up the next day.

"Please do, R.V.," said Irene. "I'll ask Donald to pick you up. Ten o'clock?"

"Half past nine would be better."

"Half past nine, then. That will be lovely."

THREE

I

Davie was sitting at the big library table, Robert's table. There was nothing further to do. At nine o'clock he had called at Blizzard and Harbottle. At half past nine he had been on the steps of the Ottery Arms, waiting for Donald. At a quarter to ten they had arrived at Cadleigh. Irene had met them at the front door. Davie had felt embarrassed. It was not possible to forget the last time he had seen them together. It was not quite fair. They did not know he was a sharer in their secret.

And now it was eleven o'clock and Davie was sitting at the big library table. There was nothing further to do. He sat there, staring at the bowl of roses, smoothing against his hand the blade of an ivory paper-knife.

Robert, Irene, Donald, Adam Merrick; the scent of the flowers; the coolness of the ivory. Maybe it is not possible to think of two things at once. But you can think about one thing and experience another. He could think about Irene and be aware of the scent of the roses. He could think about Merrick and enjoy the cold caress of the ivory. It was speculations like these, he reflected, which produced boring doctoral theses.

And then the library clock chimed the quarter and changed the subject. Glancing about him, Davie perceived a minute disarrangement at the far end of the room. A cupboard door. The lower ranges of the bookcases were built as cupboards. Large, flat publications lived there, notebooks, maps and prints in big portfolios. The door of one of these cupboards was partly open, and since Davie liked books to be level and doors to be shut, he got up and walked across the room to shut it. And then, before he did shut it, he was distracted again, for, according to habit, he had to look at the books on the shelf above the cupboard, and there, staring him in the eye, was Curzon's *Monasteries of the Levant,* and naturally he had to take it down and look for those agonizing descriptions of being drawn up the precipice in a net—the only way of approaching these rock fortresses. It always turned Davie's bones to jelly. He was not good at precipices.

All the time he was standing there reading he still remained aware of the roses. Yards away they were, but the scent was pervasive. And then, when he had shut the book and put it back on the shelf and had concentrated for a second on the scent, he recognized that it was not the roses after all; nice, but not roses. Not flowers at all, really, he thought, as he bent down to shut the cupboard door. But it would not shut, and so Davie went down on one knee and peered inside.

A small square of linen was wedged between the door and the floor of the cupboard—a handkerchief. And the scent was the scent of the handkerchief—Irene's handkerchief. Well, the house was hers, the cupboards were hers—why not her handkerchief, there or anywhere else? No reason at all, if it had not been for those nagging questions, started by Robert's notebook, nourished by Giles's doubts. Irene had been looking for something. Davie knew what was in the cupboards. There was nothing there of special interest to her. What had she been looking for?   ,

He stood up, and, taking the handkerchief with him, went back to the big table, the roses, and the paper-knife. If he had never opened that drawer, he was thinking, if he had never opened that notebook, he would not be harbouring the contradictory suspicions which now invaded his heart. Why had Robert been troubled by the death of Adam Merrick? Why had Irene been troubled, though only briefly, by the discovery of the notebook? The young man, Giles Gifford, had uncovered a secondary set of troubles. The original troubles had started here, at Cadleigh. He had not begun to understand why.

Presently he came downstairs. The garden door was open, the terrace full of sunshine. The white cat was still enjoying her summer residence behind the clump of crane's-bill in the long border. Davie crouched down to talk to her. "This," he said, "is pure vanity, Blanche. You think you go well with that wonderful Victorian magenta, don't you, eh?" And Blanche, by making one of those noiseless miaows which indicate abandonment to joy, more or less replied that she did think so. "A harmless vice, dear Blanche," said Davie. "I suffer from it badly myself."

"R.V.!"

Irene was coming towards him along the terrace with a great bunch of sweet peas in her hands. Davie pulled himself up and heard his knees creak beneath him. "A pox upon it!" he said. "I'm as stiff as old boots, but I had to discuss the amenities with Blanche."

"That's Tidwell St. Peter's," said Irene. "Everyone lives to be a hundred and two here, but most of them can't move after the age of ninety."

"Damn it, I've only been here four days."

"Have you finished, R.V.? In the library?"

"I think so. Everything was so neatly arranged I didn't have any trouble."

"And you're off tomorrow?"

"Yes, but of course I'll be back. As you know, I'd like to ask Geoffrey Willow to have a look at the anthropological stuff, but I'll take the autobiography with me, if I may. I don't suppose it will need any editing, but if it does, I can attend to it better at Cambridge."

"Do take it. I hope you'll find it's all right. I typed it."

"That's an art I have never acquired. By the way, is this yours?" He took the handkerchief out of his pocket.

"Yes—where was it?"

"In the library."

For a moment she hesitated. Then, "I was up there last night, looking for—well, anything personal. I thought there might be diaries."

"I've not seen any. I always thought Robert didn't write them."

"Perhaps not. I just didn't want personal things left about. Like that notebook. Where is it, by the way?"

"It went back to the hotel in my pocket."

"Please don't let anyone else see it, R.V."

"No, of course I won't."

"Don't you think you ought to tear it up?"

"If you wish it, Irene."

"Yes, I think I do. That's all forgotten. I don't know why Robert had to trouble himself about it."

It was a strange conversation, Davie thought. The gong for luncheon was welcome.

II

At half past two Davie was removed from the precincts of Cadleigh Abbey as suddenly and as neatly as though he had been attached to some projectile addressed to outer space. Donald had kindly offered to drive him back. Davie, who had never driven a car in his life, found speed exhilarating. He knew nothing of danger and always trusted his drivers, except when they went the wrong way, and so "Why this road?" he asked when, halfway down the drive, Donald unexpectedly turned to the right.

"I want you to see my lodge," said Donald.

Half a minute later they reached the gates, erected in 1750 by that same Sir Robert so warmly recommended on his memorial in West Tidwell Church.

Beyond them lay a Devonshire lane untouched by improvement. The high hedges had not been guillotined for the benefit of bad drivers. The wild flowers had not been poisoned by agricultural experiment. The foxgloves had not been torn up to die next day in some suburban jampot. Davie could hardly believe his eyes. It looked as it had looked in 1905, and that meant 1805 and possibly 1705. It is only recently that the far west has succumbed to the pleasures of progress.

"There you are," said Donald. "Regency cottage orné. A climbing rose. Dahlias, I need hardly say, in the front, and sweet peas at the back. What do you say to that?"

"I say thank you very much."

"No bath, of course."

"Naturally not. A Regency cottage did not expect such desperate expediencies."

"I do that up at the house."

"Is it permitted to look inside?"

"Do, if you wish. It's just two rooms and a kitchen and a larder. One Mrs. Trump comes in and bangs around with a broom from time to time, so it's reasonably tidy."

They walked up the path towards the roses.

"Even the rose is right," said Davie. "I bet that one isn't in any modern catalogue."

The door opened directly into the sitting room. It did not contain much furniture beyond an armchair, a radio set, and a table in the window covered with papers.

"Is that the novel?" asked Davie.

"It's nestling somewhere in the middle of all that."

"I hope you'll stick at it," said Davie. "The remarkable thing about books is that they won't write themselves."

There were pictures on the walls.

"My mother," said Donald, "with the infant me. It's extraordinary how ridiculous all fashions look thirty years on."

"And how charming they suddenly become thirty years later again."

"That one's Irene," said Donald.

It was a clear bright photograph of a young woman standing on a quay beside a moored yacht. To left and right portions of other boats were visible. In the background, beyond the masts, lay a border of hills across the water. At the bottom of the picture was written "Portoferraio 1967."

"Elba," said Davie. "I know that scene precisely. On the other side of the road there are trees and cafés and boutiques."

"Yes," said Donald.

"It's not as easy to spoil as other places. There's not enough of it. It was lunacy to suppose Napoleon would stay there."

"The bathing's good," said Donald. "But I don't suppose he did much of that. This is the kitchen and that's the bedroom—and that's the lot."

Davie pulled out his watch. "Thank you for the private view," he said. "Now I must be getting along."

Later, sitting in the lounge at the Ottery Arms, watching the clock before setting off to Pinewood, Davie was thinking that Donald had intended nothing, nothing at all. He had not expected that Davie would ask to go inside. He had not given a thought to the picture on the wall. And, if he had, he would have seen no wonder in it. But Davie was wondering considerably.

The name of the yacht immediately behind Irene was *Rachel*. Portoferraio, 1967. That would have been before her marriage to Robert.

III

Pinewood was a long, low house with a flower garden and a vegetable garden on the landward side, and on the other side the descent through pine trees and rhododendrons to the brook and the houses of Tidwell St. Peter's. The approach was up a short drive through the gardens.

It was half past three o'clock as Davie turned a bend in the drive and saw the house in front of him. The door was open, held back by something that glistened in the light. A rough lump of quartz it was, a barbaric and rather splendid doorstopper.

Like some picture of a "Dutch Interior," the open door revealed a hall, and, beyond that, another open door, and, beyond that, furniture and the glimpse of a window. Only the traditional distant figure was lacking, and this was supplied the moment Davie rang the bell, for immediately there she was, in the opening of the further doorway, the woman Giles had dared to call Clytemnestra on no evidence at all, and yet, thought Davie in the two seconds that fell between sight and speech, a woman much as he had imagined the younger Clytemnestra, in the days when Orestes and Electra were little, before the raddled afternoon of fear and guilt—a beautiful woman, clear-cut, determined, hard. Bother Giles! he thought. He ought to have more sense.

"Come in," said Rachel Merrick. "I expect you are Dr. Davie. Mr. Blizzard rang up."

"Yes, I am, and, if I may, I would like to see the house. It's in a lovely position."

"You know Tidwell St. Peter's?"

"Yes, indeed. I used to live here when I was a boy, but that was long ago. I haven't been here for ages. This house wasn't built in my time."

"I'll show you round upstairs first, and we can end up in the drawing room. The view is the great thing; five rooms get this sight of the bay through the pine trees."

Mrs. Merrick led him through a chintzy bedroom to a wide window.

"There!"

"Yes, it's marvellous—what my bedmaker in Cambridge would very oddly call 'a picture.'"

Mrs. Merrick was a good saleswoman, dramatic in that as in anything else. And Davie was a good customer. He loved seeing over houses and other people's possessions, and he never failed to admire the things that pleased him. "I want that," he would say, and Mrs. Merrick, who also liked pretty things, was pleased by her visitor.

"This is *the* room," she said, ushering Davie into the drawing room.

Davie walked to the window and said "Ah," walked to one end of the room and said, "I love a long room," walked to the other and came to a stand by the open hearth.

"Elba?" he said, pointing to the chunks of coloured stone.

"Why, yes," said Mrs. Merrick. "Do sit down. You've been there?"

"Some time ago," said Davie. "But one doesn't forget the colours. Somewhere I've read that there are a hundred and fifty minerals in the rocks of Elba. Are there a hundred and fifty minerals? I'm not knowledgeable about such things. Everyone who goes there brings some back. The poor island is being removed, literally stone by stone. I don't blame *you*. I've done it myself. I see your finest specimen is doing duty at the front door."

Rachel Merrick blushed—as people will, surprised by comment harmless but unexpected; it is a defensive reaction. The colour suited her.

"You're very observant."

"And you are very original. Many people in Tidwell St. Peter's prop their doors open with a stone from the beach. I've never thought that very elegant. The stones belong to the beach. They look a bit silly on a doorstep. A beach stone suggests bathing towels and sandshoes and thermos flasks. And buns," added Davie after a brief pause. "Thermos flasks and buns. We used to have things called farthing buns, four a penny, and you got thirteen instead of twelve—a baker's dozen. Isn't it strange to think about it now? But that's really why I don't like a beach stone on the doorstep. It's not a domesticated thing. It goes with the thermos flask and the buns."

"I see you are an authority on beach etiquette," said Mrs. Merrick.

"Certainly I am—as it used to be, that is. Times change. In my father's day there were different bits of beach for different modesties, a ladies' beach, a mixed bathing beach—very dashing that—a gentlemen's beach, and, if you didn't want to wear a bathing dress, you could go a long way up the beach and do just that. It's a reasonable thing to do on the sea shore. Today you'd probably be arrested. Yet you

can take all your clothes off on the stage nowadays—
which is far less reasonable—and no one cares a hang.
How very peculiar we all are."

Dr. Davie could have gone on talking about the
beach for a long time, and he had been talking for
as long as he had because it enabled him to have
a look at Mrs. Merrick. She was a bit of a stone herself, he guessed. She was handsome, but her eyes had
flint in them. He reckoned that Rachel Merrick was
hard. He reckoned she had her own way most of the
time. He reckoned she could attract men and keep
them. Like Clytemnestra, damn it.

Mrs. Merrick got up and opened a drawer in a
Regency table. "Here are some pictures of the house
and garden, taken this spring," she said. "Did you
understand that the small bit at the east end is
divided off? The house was too big for us, so we
made a little four-roomed cottage. One has to do
that sort of thing nowadays. It's let to a Miss Gonzago, but she's always out. She runs a sort of curio
shop in the village."

Colour photographs—Davie sorted them out on his
knee. Daffodils by the brook—evidently before the
creation of Stubbings's water garden. Camellias just
coming into bloom. A wistaria on the southeast front
of the house. The other side of the house with a
man standing beside the front door.

"My husband," said Mrs. Merrick.

She did not say any more. Davie looked carefully
at the picture. Short, dark, and dapper—it was interesting to see what Adam Merrick had been like.

"Thank you very much," he said, getting up. "It's
a lovely house. I must think about it very hard."

"Blizzard and Harbottle have all the details," said Mrs. Merrick. "Goodbye."

As he walked back along the drive, Davie sorted his thoughts and found himself none the wiser. It was vaguely interesting to find that that chunk of Elba quartz at the front door had not been so used until recently. According to the photograph, in the spring of the year the doorstop had been a beach stone like anyone else's. Or not quite like anyone else's. It was a stone well chosen, as the stones from Elba had been well chosen, with a handsome line of white streaking across its diameter. There it was by the door, and beside the beach stone Adam Merrick, and beside Adam Merrick a clump of daffodils.

Descending the steep hill to the village, Davie did not ponder the matter because it had any significance for him; it had none. It revolved in his mind because of his untimely lecture on the use of beach stones. Mrs. Merrick, perhaps feeling herself rebuked, had not said a word. It was absurd.

It was also a quarter past four: time for tea and a doze in the Ottery garden by the cliff. He was due at Arthur Parsley's at six.

IV

Giles was there first. When Davie arrived the car was waiting in the lane. Davie halted at the gate and looked about him. Rose Cottage stood a little back from the road, the lawn divided by a path sunk between two banks, overgrown with creeping plants and crowned with lavender. At the gate, where the banks merged with the hazel hedge, there were two short pillars made from beach stones and mortar. This reminded Davie of beach stones all over again, and for a moment he hesitated, thinking how much he disliked the stones away from the beach. They obtruded a surburban look on the lane. Firmly mortared in, they looked prim and ugly. Loose, they looked shabby. The top stone of this right hand pillar was loose. It wobbled in its setting when Davie put his hand on it. He was against Arthur Parsley's gate, but greatly in favour of his garden.

He opened the gate and walked up the path.

Rose Cottage, as Arthur Parsley had told him, was covered with roses. The roof was thatched. The windows were askew. It looked like a slightly sinister illustration to a fairy story.

He tapped on the open door, and "Come in!" called Arthur Parsley. "Here it is, beams and all. What will you have? Giles says whisky."

"Giles says too much. But thank you, yes."

"And water," said Giles.

Arthur Parsley handed the drinks. "And here are the snowstorms," he said. "Twenty-five of them. They give one a vicious sort of pleasure, don't you think? We in the warm, and all those poor creatures eternally trapped in the snow." Arthur shook one of the glass globes. "There you are. Two wretched children hurrying to school—caught again. Will they never learn?"

"But the weather clears," said Davie, watching the white flakes subside. "It may be weeks before it breaks again. I always like to think that there are days when they get to school without disaster."

"I like their amateurishness," said Arthur Parsley, turning the scholars around with an appraising eye. "They're so roughly made. The drama wouldn't be half so convincing if the characters were dainty little creatures from Chelsea or Meissen."

"Chelsea or Meissen people would never allow themselves to be caught in the snow," said Giles.

Davie moved along the row, peering.

"Hullo!" he said, picking one up that was different from the rest. "What's this? It's too light."

"Modern one. Isn't it beastly?"

"It's typical of our age. Not solid."

Davie shook it. Two boys with long hair and guitars stood in the falling snow.

"I like the boys," said Davie. "Each age has its symbols: The village maiden and the jolly jack tar for 1800; for today, long-haired boys playing guitars. But I hate the feel of the thing and the weightlessness."

"So do I. Unfortunately I was given it."

"Ah. Now this," said Davie, gently creating a storm in a country churchyard, "this is lovely. We shan't ever get things like this again. You said amateurishness. The point is that all the arts have become more professional than they used to be. Think of the musical parties that used to be given right into the twenties—"

"Sorry," said Arthur Parsley. "I wasn't born till 1930. But I know there were such things."

"Indeed there were. You 'brought your music'— boldly if you were confident of being asked to perform, furtively if you were not—and thought no shame in singing popular ballads to the stumbling accompaniment of some other brazen visitor with whom you had never practised. The B.B.C. killed all that.

An amateur music party today has to be pretty expert. The great age of the amateur is over."

"The nineteenth century?"

"Precisely. That was the time—the time when it was the recognized thing for politicians to consume their leisure hours in making a plodding translation of the *Odyssey* or the *Aeneid,* and when country clergymen wrote anthems, and even oratorios, which were presumably never performed. One of my grandfathers, Canon Tremble by splendid name, spent thirty years in the creation of an oratorio based on the life and works of the prophet Elisha, and got it published too, no doubt at his own expense. My sister and I used to pick it out on the piano when we were young. There was an admirable chorus of mocking children for sopranos and altos—'Go up, go up, thou Baldhead! Go up! Go up! Go up!'—with the opprobrious 'Baldhead' reiterated over half a dozen pages of the score to a background of ha-ha-has. One was certainly made to realize how gravely the prophet had been provoked. There was also a memorable 'March of the Bears,' though I'm afraid I no longer remember it."

"Pity," said Arthur Parsley.

"I have always taken great pleasure in the absurdity of libretti," said Davie. "Music has some power to make nonsense reasonable. In ordinary prose a Druid priestess who has had two sons by a Roman soldier would hardly dare at a solemn ceremony to invoke the goddess of chastity. But in music she can and does, and at considerable length, and the hypocrisy is happily accepted—partly, I suppose, because the words are usually shrouded 'in the decent obscurity of a learned language,' like the more startling of Gibbons's footnotes in *The Decline and Fall of the Roman Empire*."

"It has always seemed to me extremely unfair," said Arthur Parsley, "that only the classical scholar should be permitted to enjoy those entertainments. The time has come for a new edition suited to this age. Won't you undertake it?"

"Not I."

"I like Canon Tremble excessively," said Giles. "Did he find time to minister to his flock in between the labours of composition?"

"I think so. The flock was not a large one. He was vicar of Tidwell Parva for about forty years."

"Dr. Davie's family comes from these parts," said Giles to Arthur Parsley.

"Yes, I was born here."

"Would you like to come back?" asked Arthur Parsley.

"I'm pretty well stuck at Cambridge—but sometimes I think I'd like to end up here. Indeed I even went to look at a furnished house this afternoon, to let for the autumn and winter. Pinewood. You know it, I expect."

And there we are, thought Davie, in the sudden silence that followed; it's been a long circuitous journey, but we've got there at last. Pinewood.

"Yes, of course I do," said Arthur Parsley. "Did you see the famous Mrs. Merrick?"

"Certainly. She showed me round. She didn't say anything, but I understand that she lost her husband in tragic circumstances last April."

"Yes. It was a pretty odd business, but nobody ever found any dirty evidence. And so they brought in an open verdict. It was, I suppose, an accident." Very deliberately he picked up a globe containing a ship set upon waves of stormy plaster, shook it violently and created a major calamity. "It's nice, isn't it?" he said.

For a moment Davie feared that Mr. Parsley had been diverted from the purpose to which he had been so carefully led. " 'O hear us when we cry to thee!' " Mr. Parsley sang softly as he returned the snowstorm to its shelf, " 'For those in peril on the sea.' " Then he sat down and gazed at Davie, as though in search of a change of conversation.

But Arthur Parsley, it presently appeared, had created the diversion with deliberate dramatic purpose.

"To a small extent," he said, after a long pause, "I was a material witness. You see, the entrance to Quarry View—or Gonville Lodge, as he calls it—is just round the corner from here, so my back garden and Stubbings's front garden are alongside. I had gone to Exeter that day—by bus—and I had been glad to accept a lift home from Robert Cassillis. I'd asked him in for a drink, and we were sitting in the back parlour when Adam Merrick came storming up to Quarry View to tell Stubbings what he thought about his idiotic water garden. Cassillis got up at once and said he didn't want to listen to it, and he hadn't meant to stay anyhow. So he went, got into his car and drove off down the hill. I had to see him to the door, but I didn't go down to the gate. I nipped back to the garden as soon as I could. Not sharing Sir Robert's scruples, I wanted to hear the fun. And I did. It was mostly Adam. First of all he let fly a load of abuse about diverting the stream, and Ernest Stubbings couldn't find anything to say because he must have known he was in the wrong, and being chairman of the parish council it wasn't the sort of mistake he ought to have made. He made a shot at blustering it out and said it was a lot of fuss about nothing and that the dam would be removed next day as soon as Challice had finished the islands. And then Merrick said if the dam wasn't removed by ten o'clock he'd summons him, and then Stubbings told him to get out and never darken his door again."

"How fine! Did he actually use that famous phrase?"

"Yes, he did. And then Adam Merrick said something very odd. He said—of course I haven't got the exact words—'You and your lobsters! Think that out, and get that dam down by ten o'clock.'

"And then he stumped out of the garden with never another word from Ernest Stubbings. Then I heard Adam Merrick go down the lane towards the path by the quarry—the path to his own property. And then I thought I heard someone run down the lane after him. But it was dark by that time. I didn't see anyone."

"Did you tell all that to the coroner?" asked Davie.

"Most of it, but not Adam's last remark. It didn't seem to make sense when one repeated it."

It made a sort of sense to Davie, but he did not say anything except, "What a business!"

"Yes," said Arthur Parsley. "It was. There was a Horticultural Society committee meeting here that evening after dinner. That kept me busy till late, so I didn't know anything about it, of course, till next day when Rachel came round to tell me, early. I was still having breakfast. She was terribly distressed, but she pulled herself together remarkably well. I took her down to the gate, but she wouldn't let me see her home. She always did have a great sense of—how shall I say?—situation."

"It's a gift of drama, really," said Giles. "Mrs. Merrick can't help taking a part, as it were."

"On this occasion," said Davie, "that was appropriate. She was the widow. I gather she did it well."

"She did," said Arthur Parsley. "Do have another drink."

"No, thank you. I must be going. Thank you for the snowstorms. May I shake one more?"

"Do."

"Well, this one then: a snowman in the snow. That's not cruel. It's his favourite weather."

Arthur Parsley took them to the door.

"Many thanks. I hope we'll meet again," said Davie. "Are you on the telephone?"

"Yes, too often I am," said Parsley, scribbling on a small pad which lay on the hall table. "Here you are. Tidwell 432. Do give me a ring some time, or just bob in."

"Thank you."

"I'll give you a lift," said Giles.

"That was entertaining," said Davie a minute later. "I've always adored snowstorms. And now what can you tell me about our host?"

"Nothing at all. He's a gentleman at leisure."

"That's rare."

"Well, he's lived at Rose Cottage for about five years and no one's ever seen him do a stroke, except in the garden, where, I must say, he does a good many."

"And he's how old?"

"He said he was born in 1930."

"So he did. Fortunate Mr. Parsley."

Giles swung the car to a halt beside the hotel steps. Davie hauled himself out. "I've never been able to get out of a car," he grumbled. "Or into one. They're all designed wrong. Or I am. That's it. Thanks. Well—goodbye, Giles, and thank you. I'm off to London in the morning."

"I hope you're going to come back, Dr. Davie."

"I'll have to come back, and, when I do, we'll meet."

Giles fumbled in his pocket. "Here's that newspaper report," he said. "I hope you haven't given up this business, sir."

"I don't know—truly I don't know. I can't say I've discovered anything particularly interesting."

"No, I suppose not. But you may. Please don't forget about it."

"I won't," said Davie, lifting a farewell hand. "Goodbye."

Except for the receptionist, the hall and the lounge were empty, everyone in the hotel being deeply involved with dinner. A quick wash and he must follow. But as he turned aside, there was Giles pushing open the glass door and waving a wisp of paper.

"You left this," he said. "Arthur P.'s telephone number."

"Thanks, but you needn't have bothered."

"You asked for it!"

"I only asked if he were on the telephone."

Giles eyed Davie suspiciously.

"You could have discovered that without asking," he said.

Davie took the piece of paper and put it in his waistcoat pocket.

"Yes, wise one, I could. But I was impatient. I suddenly wanted to know at that particular moment, while it was in my mind. Don't hold it against me. Goodbye again."

"Goodbye, Dr. Davie."

Giles had a secret smile on his face as he walked down the steps to the car. He was excited. It had occurred to the romantic youth that perhaps old Davie had not given the business up after all—though he didn't see what the hell it mattered to anyone whether Arthur Parsley was on the blower or not. Most people were. And why should old Davie have been impatient?

Puzzled but a little elated, Giles climbed into his aged car and drove it back to West Tidwell as fast as he dared. He was, as so often, a little late for dinner.

FOUR

I

As the train leaves Exeter one has to look out of the window. That is certain. The incomparable valley of the Exe is not to be exchanged for newspapers. To the right the hanging woods, to the left the weir, the water meadows and the distant hills. There are sights more spectacular, none more gently agreeable. He might not see it many times more, Davie thought, and so he looked at it until the track lost touch with the weaving river, and became more closely held between the crowding fields. Then he started on the papers.

He was not much in the habit of reading newspapers, but he liked to do so in the train, regarded it as a treat, and derived much amusement from the exercise—not, of course, from the waffling excuses and recriminations of politicians, nor from the incomprehensibilities of the money market, nor from the infinitely boring reports from the jungle world of sport. But he did enjoy the milder excitements of libel and burglary and fraud, and such-like old-fashioned entertainments. And there were the reviews of book and theater and opera, and always the hope that Jack Pincock would say the conductor had taken the *cavatina* too fast and Richard Serpent (taking a rare risk) would regret that it had been taken too slow.

After combing the papers he looked out of the window again. The White Horse of Westbury would be coming up soon and he never allowed himself to miss that.

Towns usually had advertisements near the line, but one didn't see advertisements in fields nowadays. That was a good thing, he supposed . . . and yet with what affection he remembered those two cut-out men who used to stride through the meadows bearing a plank with the legend "Hall's Distemper" written on it. What had happened to them, and what had happened to those other three men in white coats who devoted themselves to recommending Ripolin Paint? The second man was painting his message on the back of the first man, and the third man was painting his on the back of the second man. It had always worried Davie as a child that there had been nobody to paint anything on the back of the third man. Where were they now? Banished, no doubt, in some preserve-the-countryside campaign. Well yes . . . but he had been fond of them. They had stuck to their job with such dependable devotion.

Another memorable figure of the railway line was the fisherman in oilskins with the great codfish upon his back. He lived near London, and indeed still does, above the door of the Scott's Emulsion Factory.

Thought is swifter than wheels, swifter than sound. One word and the scene is changed, the years dissolved. Scott's Emulsion, thought Davie, and the railway carriage disappeared, and he was looking at Robert—Robert aged ten—pouring his cod liver oil out of the window. The fact that Miss Manger had happened to be immediately below had transformed a normal maneuver into an exquisite ceremony. And there he was where he started. Robert.

Robert, Irene, and Donald. Robert, Irene, Donald, and Adam Merrick. They had all been interested in Adam Merrick. And Adam Merrick was dead, dead of an accident in a sandstone quarry.

If it had not been for that boy Giles, Davie would have let the matter go. And rightly, he guessed. For what had he discovered that was not known to everybody else? Nothing of value. True, a photograph had suggested that Irene had known Adam Merrick longer and better than he had thought—and probably Donald Bride too. And there was Mrs. Merrick's early morning visit to Rose Cottage. Did she consider the telephone insufficiently dramatic? These things were interesting, but he had not discovered a single thing which disputed the decision of the coroner's jury.

And yet—why had Robert been disturbed enough to make those notes in the blue notebook? And why was he still carrying that notebook in the security of his breast pocket—the notebook Irene had asked him to destroy? Not choosing to answer his own questions, Davie leaned back in his corner and said to himself in the train's rhythm, Giles's mystery, not my mystery. Giles's mystery, not my mystery.

And Giles's mystery, not my mystery, thought Davie to himself when he woke up an hour later within a mile of London.

It was vexing to think he had missed the fisherman and the codfish.

II

Davie was staying at the Chesterfield Club, where he had managed to get (he usually did manage to get) his favourite bedroom at the back of the house, the room with the *toile de Jouy* paper, overlooking the garden.

By the time he had unpacked and had had a lie down (developing into a pleasant doze) and dressed again and peeped into the library and gone downstairs, it was past six o'clock. In the morning room the evening faces were gathered together. Everything was exactly as it always was. In a distant corner Frederick Dyke was hiding behind the evening paper. By the open fireplace little Willie Marchant was talking to Adrian Ballsover about the balance of payments. From his usual seat Conway Gordon was giving his familiar performance to an admiring audience. Davie disliked this entertainment. He always wanted to interrupt, and a second voice was about as welcome to Conway Gordon as an additional fool would have been to, alas, poor Yorick, setting the table in a roar at the court of Denmark.

He passed quickly on to the bar, and was happy to find George Canteloupe there, he of the magnificent belly, regaling his vast and amiable form with gin. Canteloupe was exactly the company Davie needed, and so, presently, avoiding the fellowship of the long table, they dined together in a corner and talked about old days and Robert Cassillis.

"The last time I saw Robert," said George Canteloupe, "was two summers ago—in Elba."

Knife and fork poised above a rather splendid grilled sole, Davie glanced quickly across the table, but George Canteloupe was not looking at him. He was staring down at his plate with a secretly amused smile, the smile of one who has something worth telling and is wondering how best to play it.

"It was at Portoferraio," he went on. "I had gone for a jollyo to one of the rather swell hotels near by, and I'd come in one evening to see the sights—which are fairly limited in Portoferraio, but, such as they are, are best seen from that good street that faces the harbour."

"I know."

"It really is very pretty at night, with all the yachts moored to the quay, closely side by side, and the lights in the water, and the further shore across the harbour picked out in lights—not like some gala display, but just because they happen to be there. And people dining, and people walking up and down under the trees. It is still quite simple there, not a bit spoilt. Well—there I was, sitting at a table outside a café, when up comes Robert and says, "Hullo, George! Can I join you?" just as though we'd been seeing each other every day, whereas in fact it was at least twenty years since we'd last met. So down he sat and we had a long talk about everything, you included. I shall always remember it because it was while we were talking that Robert had the first sight of the girl he was to marry so soon after."

"Irene."

"Was that her name? He was telling me about an

experience he'd had in Malaysia, when I felt that the full stream of his invention had been slightly tapped, and presently that it had been positively diverted. What had happened was that a remarkably pretty young woman, somewhere in her twenties, had sat down at the next table to ours."

"Ah."

"Robert kept glancing across at her, and then when the waiter came up, and it became obvious that the young woman was not greatly proficient in restaurant Italian, he leant forward and asked if he could help."

"A famous gambit."

"And so we got talking. It appeared that the girl came from one of the yachts in the harbour, and didn't, I thought, like it very much. And then Robert asked her to come and inspect his yacht next day —and I thought it would be tactful if I went back to my hotel. I was going on to Lucca next day. I didn't see Robert again. But I heard he married the girl three weeks later."

"And it was a huge success. It's sad their happiness lasted so short a time."

With the pudding—which was a Mont Blanc chestnut cream, out of season, and out of a tin, but not at all bad—Canteloupe told Davie about a cruise he was thinking of taking among the islands of the South Pacific.

"You alarm me exceedingly," said Davie. "Quite apart from what happened to Captain Cook, have you never heard of the South Sea Bubble? Besides, should the world turn out after all to be flat, as I have long suspected—"

"You are an absurd old man."

"So I have reason to fear," said Davie. "And now I must leave you—"

"Not coffee?"

"No. If I go into the garden I shall start talking."

"You will."

"And I have work to do upstairs."

"Robert's work?"

"Yes."

"Then I won't persuade you. I'm glad I was here tonight."

"So am I. Thanks for your company. Good night, George."

And so Davie went upstairs to his bedroom, collected the three typewritten volumes of Robert's biography, took three steps along the corridor and entered the library. There was nobody else there.

He crossed to the window and looked down on the garden, where his fellow members of the Chesterfield Club sat drinking their coffee and talking. It was entertaining to observe this congregation of middle-aged men, gossiping and giggling, for that was what they were doing. It all sounded delightfully silly. From a neighbouring room the talk was punctuated by a frivolous click of billiards balls.

Well, well, thought Davie, God bless us all. Then he gave up eavesdropping, retired to a deep armchair, adjusted a green-shaded lamp, set two of the volumes of typescript on a small table at his side, and took the other in his hands. The early part of the book he had read at Cadleigh. Naturally he had: there was a lot about himself in it. This evening he meant to run through the whole book, just turning the pages over, learning the shape of it, seeing if

Robert had left any instructions, any notes about possible illustrations.

Certainly Davie had not meant to settle down to read the book, but again and again his attention was engaged by some passage or other, and then he would spend minutes with one of Robert's encounters with Tibetan shepherds, Kurdish brigands or Greek Orthodox monks. What with one thing and another it was nearly eleven o'clock before he started on the third volume. And it was ten past eleven when he found the pieces of paper in Robert's handwriting. They were tucked in between pages sixty-four and sixty-five of the typescript.

At first he thought the sheets were a draft of some addition, some insertion to be made at this place. But the first sentence removed that impression. "I am involved in a mystery—because of this Adam Merrick." It was then that Davie lifted his head and stared at the clock, and saw that it was ten past eleven.

Because of this Adam Merrick. There had always seemed something peculiar about the argument in the blue notebook. Davie had recognized that from the first, but it was only now that he suddenly comprehended the nature of that peculiarity. Robert had not been investigating the tragedy with a detective's zeal to uncover a solution. He had been making those notes because he was afraid about something. Had he feared to find a solution in case it might implicate Irene? Had he been trying to assure himself that she could not have been involved? If so, the blue notebook had not sufficed. Here he seemed to be trying again, to be setting down in greater detail all that he understood of some dangerous complication. "I am involved in a mystery." It was obvious why the notes had been put where Davie had found them. It was the best possible place of concealment. Locks have keys. Drawers and boxes can be investigated. But who would think of ruffling through a bound typescript on a bookshelf? Least of all Irene, who had done the typing, and certainly never wanted to see it again—not in that form. Robert was not expecting to die. From day to day the typescript was the safest safe in the house. And, if anything did happen to Robert, the book would go to his literary executor. It would be equally safe with Davie.

Twelve past eleven. He put the volume of typescript down on the table. Then he began to read.

III

I am involved in a mystery because of this Adam Merrick.

At about a quarter to seven on the night Merrick died I was at Arthur Parsley's. I had given him a lift from Exeter. We were having a drink in his back parlour, the evening mild and the window open. His back garden lies against Stubbings's front garden and suddenly we heard a tremendous argument going on at Stubbings's front door. It was Merrick in a fury about something Stubbings had done to the brook. I didn't want to listen and I was in a hurry anyhow and so I left. It was getting dark—especially here where the trees arch across the road. I got in the car, passed the brook, and had just started up the hill when my lights failed. It was a fuse. I had to get out and jigger about. Eventually I got them going, and in the sudden illumination I saw a man crossing the road into Merrick's wood. It was certainlv Donald Bride. There's a path there that leads to Merrick's house and ultimately to the public road, but I couldn't think why he would be going that way at that time of night. I had business in West Tidwell, but I got back at a quarter to eight. Irene was as usual—but rather quiet during dinner.

After dinner she went up to her room for something, and just then the telephone rang. I must have picked it up in the drawing room at the precise moment that Irene answered it upstairs. Before I could speak I heard Donald say "Irene?" "Yes." Then, "Have you heard?" Donald said. "They've found him—" "Adam?" "Yes. He'd fallen over the edge of the quarry. He's dead." I didn't want to eavesdrop—but I didn't want to be heard hanging up. He didn't say much more. I waited for the click from upstairs before putting my receiver back.

A few mintues later Irene came in. I said, "Who was ringing?" And she answered without embarrassment, "Donald. He wanted to tell us there's been an accident at the quarry. Adam Merrick has fallen over the edge. I understand he's dead."

She was not concealing a thing. But there were two things that hit me in the mind. What had Donald been doing in Merrick's woods? And why had Donald said, "They've found him," as though Irene must know whom he meant. And as I thought about that my mind went back to the time when we got back from our tour, last October. Irene had been in great spirits all the time until the day old Miss Fraser-Dandridge called on us and gave a dissertation on everything that had happened in Tidwell St. Peter's in the last twelve months. Of course Irene didn't know any of the people she was talking about but she made a shot at sounding interested. Then, just as the old lady was getting up to go, she said, "But I haven't told you about Pinewood. It's been taken by a Mr. and Mrs. Merrick. Delightful people. He is fond of the sea and sails in the Mediterranean. Mr. Adam Merrick. One does not often hear the name Adam."

And so she gathered up her numerous belongings and tottered out to her car.

When I got back to the drawing room Irene was standing looking out of the window.

I said, "Calling's out of fashion—but there are some things one has to do. Pinewood is the neighbouring estate. You'll have to call, Irene."

She turned round and I was surprised to see that she was terribly pale. She said, "No, Robert. Don't ask me to go calling on people. I can't do it." I said, "I'm afraid they'll think you rather rude." And she said, "I can't help it. *You* call, Robert." It wasn't a matter to argue out—at least not then. And so I did call. And Mrs. Merrick was polite enough (for these days) to return the call. But Irene was out.

It was soon after that call that Irene lost her spirits. She seemed to worry about something. She would go off by herself in the woods. Once I found her reading a letter she obviously didn't want me to see. I did not connect this with Adam Merrick then, but now I do. I can't help noticing that her spirits revived immediately after his death. It is my spirits that are failing. I can't ask her, but I must know what happened. Donald was in the wood the night Merrick died. Irene knew he was there. Was anyone else there?

I am not making these notes in the hope of solving a crime (it may not be a crime: the police did not think it was), but because I want to persuade myself that Irene could not have had anything to do with it, supposing there had been a crime. I have always written things down. It helps clear the mind. This is July. The inquest at the end of March did not resolve my problems. I suppose I ought to chuck it. I went today for the fourth time to look at the old quarry. It tells me nothing at all. Coming out I ran into Stubbings. He wanted to know what I was up to. He is the most inquisitive creature—sham-jovial and damned familiar. I said I was reviving old memories. I used to play games there with R.V. He said he'd seen me there before and it didn't do to be sentimental. We all had to grow old. It is very difficult to move in this little place without everyone knowing exactly where you've been.

Naturally I have not mentioned these things to anyone else, though I did discreetly ask Arthur Parsley if he thought an accident was the true explanation of Merrick's death. He looked surprised. I suppose that was natural. To ask a man if he has doubts is to suggest one has doubts oneself. He said, "You mean suicide? I don't think so. Why should he?" But of course I hadn't meant suicide.

I can't get rid of this doubt in my heart. Am I like Othello?

There was a date at the end of the paper. It was only two days before Robert's death. For the first time there came into Davie's mind an unwelcome thought. Had Robert's love for Irene—his anxiety for her reputation—unhinged his mind? If his happiness had been destroyed by the discovery of evil, might he have preferred to leave this world rather than live with it? That would not have been like the man Davie had known as a boy. But old men grow foolish.

The clock on the mantelshelf struck twelve. Davie put the papers in his pockets, gathered the books under his arm, crossed to the door and put out the light. Put out the light, he said under his breath, and stood a moment in the darkness, pondering why Robert had compared himself to Othello. Othello had been jealous of Cassio. Had he, perhaps, failed to write down all that was in his heart?

Then Davie opened the door, stepped into the lighted corridor, and stopped there a moment to look, as he always did, at a picture of a splendid Mandarin duck, lecherously eyeing his submissive lady. It was as great a study of character as of feathers.

Five minutes later he was in bed, his mind troubled, but not suffering from the excitement which follows discovery. He could sleep.

The next day he took an early train to Cambridge.

IV

Cambridge in July is beautiful and peaceful. The Long Vacation is on, which means that some undergraduates are in residence, but only those with spe-

cial work to do. It is a time for tennis, a time for
punts and canoes, but not for crews and bumping
races.

Davie took a taxi from the station. It is a long
way to the colleges. Just as the first women's college
had been built at some distance from Cambridge for
the more certain protection of the young ladies from
the lascivious attentions of the young gentlemen, so,
likewise the Cambridge railway station had been sited
by the careful Victorians as far away as possible from
the university. They had to keep up with the times,
but they knew that it would bring contamination,
not only through dirt and noise, but also it was to
be feared, in the form of undesirable visitors. It
would certainly be a good plan to make the railway
as inconvenient as possible.

It was prim, but it was this crafty stroke of moral-
ity which had brought to Cambridge its greatest bless-
ing and amenity, and it was this Victorian exclusive-
ness which now caused Dr. R. V. Davie, fellow of
St. Nicholas's College, to hire himself a taxi. As he
sped down St. Andrew's Street he recalled how, in
his undergraduate days and indeed for several years
after, he had chosen to take twice as long, riding
in a glorious hansom cab. People always think of a
hansom as a delight of the Naughty Nineties and
of the Edwardians. But in declining numbers they
lasted certainly into the nineteen twenties, and one
or two of them had always been waiting at the Cambridge railway station, competing with the primitive
taxis. That memory of being driven in a hansom was
one small compensation for being old—so Davie was
thinking as his cab drew up at the entrance to the
college in St. Nicholas Lane.

NO CASE FOR THE POLICE 101

He left his luggage by the outer gate and made his way down the Long Walk, carrying the three volumes of typescript under his arm. Dark red seventeenth-century walls flanked the broad paved way, sheltering from the vulgar gaze the Master's garden on the one side, and the Fellows' garden on the other. Snapdragons flowered unbidden from crevices on the top of the wall.

Mr. Jump, the head porter, was on duty at the Lodge. Davie asked him to arrange for the transport of his cases, and Mr. Jump, with a graceful inclination of his beaky nose, undertook to supervise this operation as soon as he could procure the services of a suitable underling.

Mrs. Pilsworthy, one of the elder members of the corps of bedmakers, was hanging up her keys on her way out of college. Davie was always glad to see Mrs. Pilsworthy, because she belonged to the old school and wore a remarkable straw hat with a ruche of blue ribands around it. Bedmakers of today may wear a scarf, but rarely so fossilized a thing as a hat. In Davie's undergraduate days hats for bedmakers had been a sign of their office. A few of the especially ancient ones had even worn bonnets.

Mrs. Pilsworthy's hat (which she had certainly worn for at least twenty years) was a link, so Davie felt, between old and new, and would assuredly deserve a mention in the *History of Bedmaking,* a research exercise which he always hoped would be undertaken before it was too late by some eager candidate for a Ph.D.

And so Davie had a smile for Mrs. Pilsworthy and enquired how she did, and Mrs. Pilsworthy told him,

adding however that she mustn't complain and that
there were others worse than her.

"Yes, indeed," said Davie. "And, speaking for myself, I always find that a great comfort. Good morning, Mrs. Pilsworthy."

"Good morning, Dr. Davie."

"Your cases will be round as soon as I can find
Tom," said Mr. Jump, and "Thank you, Mr. Jump,"
said Davie.

And so, the civilities accomplished, Davie walked
on under the great towered gateway, and beheld with
accustomed delight the immaculate lawn, and the
modest Jacobean buildings, fringed with flowers.
There was no one about.

A smaller archway, in the corner of the court, took
him into Baxter's Court. His staircase, M, was on
the far side. On his left, as he walked down the paved
path, was the Dutch garden. In one form or another
it had been there for three hundred years. It was
odd to think that he had known it for a sixth of
that time. When Davie had first entered the college
there had been an ancient don who had come to
St. Nicholas's in 1840. Put me and old Pickering end
to end, thought Davie, and we'd add up to half the
age of the garden. Three hundred years is nothing
in a place like this—nothing at all.

V

Davie had had several reasons for coming to Cambridge. The college was his home. He wanted to de-
posit Robert's autobiography in the safety of his

rooms. And on this particular night he had promised to attend a performance of *As You Like It,* which by permission of the Master and Fellows was to be given under the greenwood tree in a corner of the Close. The universities nowadays are dedicated to the drama. Not a college but has its society. Not a society that does not march with the *avant garde.* Indeed in student circles the *avant garde* of the theater forms so powerful a contingent that it is difficult to discern any main body behind it. Everyone leads the way.

As You Like It certainly seemed an unfashionable choice. Davie connected the play with school speech days. But he had not seen it for years and he venerated the words. *As You Like It,* under the trees, in the cool of a July night: it sounded delicious.

"You amaze me, Davie," said Cowl at dinner in hall. Cowl was lean and cynical, and Davie, who was neither, was much attached to him. "You imagine you are going to see a play by William Shakespeare. You are behind the times. I was betrayed into seeing a performance of *Macbeth* recently. Somehow they had figured out that that nervous man was an unmitigated villain, and that Lady Macbeth was his unwilling accomplice. But how about 'We will proceed no further with this business,' you were about to ask—"

"Well—"

"Ah-ha! Macbeth only said that to test her. Everything has to be new nowadays, Davie. Everything has to be different, and as for what the author actually *intended*—"

"Actors have always had difficulties about that. Apart from her own scenes, Mrs. Porter, Garrick's

Lady Macbeth, is said never to have read the play."

"Ha!" Cowl's scorn reduced the shade of Mrs. Porter to a frazzle.

"I remember once hearing a King Lear pronounce the famous words, 'Let copulation thrive,' and quite suddenly gaining the impression that he didn't know the meaning of the word 'thrive.' It was a very odd sensation."

"You are an old knave," said Cowl.

"I take it you are not coming to the play."

"Certainly not. It is mathematically certain to be an intolerable bore."

"Ah well," said Davie. "I like new readings. If they're no good they soon disprove themselves. I trust our vulgar laughter will not disturb you."

And so, presently, he made his way to the Close, wearing an overcoat and bearing a rug. July was behaving splendidly, but it was not likely to be hot in the open air after ten o'clock.

He found his seat in the front row, settled himself down, looked about him, and was suddenly surprised. On the open greensward, bowered in trees as old as Arden, an evil-looking motor car was parked. Davie perceived that he had misjudged the young men of St. Nicholas's College. They were as much in the van as everyone else. And thank God they were punctual. A laurestinus bush broke into rhythm—a drum, a saxophone, a guitar. The play began.

It appeared that the elder son of Sir Roland de Boys was a minor sort of hoodlum, but outclassed by the usurping duke, the reigning gangster of that manor, under whose sinister direction the wrestling match was thrillingly all-in, the clothes as near as dammit all off. It was all very disquieting, and when

the car drove away it was loaded with hoods bran-
dishing sub-machine guns.

But meantime down in the forest something stirred.
It was a lover and his lass. It was a whole crowd of
them. For Arden concealed not only the banished
duke and his few companions, but also a congregation of happy hippies with shells and laces round
their necks and feathers in their hair, snapping guitars to a portable microphone and belting out im-
mortal lines with unfamiliar manners. And, over all,
Jaques, in a baggy suit, smoking a pipe, gloomed like
some superannuated lecturer from the London School
of Economics. *As You Like It* had become a contemporary work—but the words were still Shakespeare's,
and the extraordinary and exciting thing was that
they sounded right. Sweet are the uses of adversity.
Davie was enormously impressed.

And when the show came to an end, the music
played on in the laurestinus bush—drum, saxophone
and guitar—and suddenly the actors ran among the
spectators, enticing them to come and dance, which
the younger members of the audience were very happy to do. But, "I won't dance, thank you," said Davie
to the amiable youth who endeavoured to persuade
him to make a fool of himself. "I read in the papers
only yesterday that nothing is so frequent a cause
of coronary thrombosis in the aged as violent and
unexpected exercise. I'm afraid I *am* aged as far as
my arteries go, but my heart is with you. Good night,
and my thanks to all of you."

"Thanks very much," said the young man. "I'll tell
them." And off he ran in pursuit of a young woman,
who capitulated without any conditions at all.

Davie picked his way among the trees back to the

college. But what about the winter and rough weather, he was thinking. I could never take that. And
what about the food? There had been an admirable
dish of sweetbreads at dinner, cooked in white wine.
How the devil would you do that in the Forest of
Arden?

In these ancient trees of the Close also there were
tongues, and sermons enough in the rosy bricks of
college buildings. "I would not change it," he said
to himself. "I would not change Baxter's Court for
all the Forest of Arden."

He was about to turn aside into M staircase when
he heard someone calling to him.

"Hi! Davie!"

The senior tutor, Max Martin, had followed him
from the Close.

"And what did you think of that?"

"God and the late Professor Bradley forgive me,
but I enjoyed it quite enormously."

"I thought you would, but I was disappointed not
to see you dancing."

"I was asked," said Davie with perceptible pride.

"And you refused?"

"Alas, yes."

"Come back to my rooms for a drink."

"Thank you. That sort of roistering is more in
my line these days."

Max Martin lived on the Hall staircase in an ancient room with beams across the ceiling painted with
medieval monograms. It was a part of the original
monastery of St. Anastasius and the Glorious Virgin
Edwina, suppressed in 1472 (for scandalous behaviour) by Bishop Allbottel, who had turned the place

into a college. When Davie looked at that ceiling he always found himself thinking, not of the piety of the builders, but of those last naughty monks behaving scandalously. Then, lowering his sights, he would look at the seventeenth century panelling, where portraits of academic predecessors hung in their golden frames. Another age, a different mystery. Port, snuff, and scholarship were there, and the foundation for a serious study of the history of wigs.

As soon as Martin had poured the drinks he said, "I'm glad you're back, Davie. I wanted to consult you about something."

"Tell on."

"You know there was trouble in one of the colleges a little time back about drugs. People had been smoking reefers at parties. It was nothing much, but enough for the police to have made enquiries. I don't think they found anything very serious. Well, it's all serious, but they didn't find evidence of what is called hard drugs. But then, a couple of days ago, our Mrs. Tuffy did. She's the bedmaker on H staircase, in the corner of the cloisters."

Davie nodded. There was no need to tell him where H staircase was.

"She went into the rooms of an undergraduate called Myrtle, and found him in a stupor. She rushed off and told Jump, and Jump stalked up here and told me, and Myrtle was removed to hospital. He'd been taking what the hippie world calls snow. The question is where did he get it from. It's difficult to get anything out of people once they're hooked, as the phrase is. For one thing they don't tell the truth. I don't want to call in the police. Nothing would come of that but scandal and newspaper reporters."

"The police would have examined his rooms," Davie pointed out. "Have you?"

"The head porter and I were both there when Myrtle was taken away. We saw nothing. Mrs. Tuffy has reported nothing."

"Have you the key?"

"Not here."

"You can get it from the lodge. Can we go and have a look at it?"

"Now?"

"Yes. It would be well to go when Mrs. Tuffy isn't about."

"It would. All right. Come along."

There are etiquettes in colleges. Normally a senior tutor would not enter an empty set of rooms without being conducted thither by the head porter. But Max Martin said, "I won't bother you, Mr. Jump. It's only a small matter. I can manage. And you can't very well leave your gate."

And Mr. Jump, who had no mind to go trailing around the college at that hour of night, was delighted to forego his privilege, so long as it was plainly agreed that that privilege existed.

So, armed with the key, Max Martin and Davie passed through the cloister arch. It was nearly midnight. Through the arcades they could see the small central lawn, half in the shadow of the chapel, half in the light of the moon. The only sound was the sound of their footsteps as, not talking, they walked down the south side of the cloister. And there, just round the corner, was the low arch leading to H staircase. Inside the arch, on the left, three names were painted in white on a black ground: G. H. Joicey, K. W. Myrtle, H. Gamble.

H staircase is the oldest in the college, framed with great beams of oak, steep and narrow, so narrow that the landing outside Myrtle's rooms will only accommodate one person. Davie waited on the stair below while Martin put the key in the lock. He did not see the door swing inwards at the pressure of a hand, but he heard him say, "The oak wasn't shut. Mrs. Tuffy must have forgotten to lock up." Then Martin crossed the threshold, and Davie, mounting the last two stairs, followed him in.

Immediately across the small hall the inner door stood open. Beyond it they could see Myrtle's room, so peaceful in the moonlight that for a couple of seconds Martin hesitated to break the charm.

Certainly, the ancient chamber looked less beautiful in artificial light. It could have been made a pretty room if undergraduates had time or money or thoughts for such effete pleasures as comfort and the contemplation of beauty. Here was the usual table with its ugly cloth, and books, books on shelves, books on the table. In the corner was a guitar in a case. On the walls were several reproductions of abstract paintings, things which no doubt reflected the taste of the man who could nevertheless put up with the hideous material which covered the two armchairs, inherited as a matter of course from the previous tenant. On the mantelshelf were a few photographs.

"It's bleak," said Davie. "Nothing to please."

"There was a—" began Martin.

"Yes?"

"I was going to say there was an ornament on the mantelshelf—but it's gone now. I noticed it because it was one of those old-fashioned snowstorms that one never sees nowadays. Only it was a modern imitation. Mrs. Tuffy wouldn't have moved it—on her bedmaker's oath she wouldn't have. I wonder what happened to it."

Davie stood still for several seconds looking fixedly at Martin's top coat button. Then he crossed the room, entered the small hall and opened the outer door.

"What are you up to now?" asked Martin, following him.

"I think," said Davie, "that this oak was not just unshut. I think it was forced."

"Forced?"

"Yes. It's bust."

"But why—"

"I don't know—unless someone wanted the only thing that according to you is missing."

"The snowstorm?"

"It's merely a suggestion. If you called the police they might find fingerprints, or they might not. If you don't call the police you can do nothing else. It is in any case difficult to call them as you didn't call them earlier."

"I don't want to call the police. This is not a great matter—I hope. But it would make a great noise."

"It would," said Davie. "I think you may have to leave it. Anyhow, let's leave it for tonight. But if you don't mean to call the police you'd better ask the bursar if he'll get the lock mended. Or Mrs. Tuffy will be raising a romance about it."

"I'm afraid that may happen anyhow. I'll go first,"

said Martin, cautiously descending the stairs. "Are you here for a bit?"

"No, I'm afraid not. I've got to go away tomorrow," said Davie, who until that moment had made no such decision.

"I'm sorry about that."

"I don't think you'll get any further evidence out of that room, Max."

"No, I suppose not."

At the foot of the Hall staircase their ways divided, and they stopped to say good night. "Thank you for coming," said Max Martin. But Davie had something on his mind. "What was this snowstorm like?" he asked.

"The snowstorm? It wasn't like the old ones, complete with scenery, and it wasn't proper china. It was a light sort of thing with two chaps inside playing guitars. But it worked. I shook it, and it snowed. Do you think it's important?"

"It could be. I don't know. But if it is important it's important somewhere else, I would think. Not here."

"That's enigmatic."

"It's just a guess."

"Well, good night."

So Martin mounted the stairs to his medieval room, and Davie walked on through the arch into Baxter's Court, where the clipped yews cast Jacobean shadows on the lawn. But Davie was not looking at the Dutch garden. He walked with his head bent down and his hands clasped in front of him—a curious monkish attitude of his, which, before now, had caused rude boys to call "Amen" from passing bicycles.

He was thinking of Rose Cottage and of Mr. Pars-

ley and of two long-haired boys playing guitars under a glass dome—and of two other long-haired boys
playing guitars under the greenwood tree in the college Close. It was all so horribly apposite.

> Here shall he see
> No enemy
> But winter and rough weather.

It would be good to think so; but he shook his
head a little, and pursed his lips, and drew his thick
eyebrows together in a frown. "Here comes a motive
to light me to bed," he whispered as he mounted
the dark stairs.

V

The next morning Davie caught the nine o'clock
train to London. In his pocket he carried the blue
notebook and the notes he had found concealed in
the typescript. But he was no longer thinking about
a dead man called Adam Merrick; he was thinking
about a half-living boy called K. W. Myrtle, and he
was angry.

The three volumes of autobiography he had left
behind in his rooms; but he had added two new
encumbrances to his luggage, and they were both
heavy. The first was his best snowstorm; he thought
Mr. Parsley would be interested in that. The other
was a leather case containing binoculars. It had occurred to him that if Mr. Ernest Stubbings could
examine Dr. R. V. Davie from a distance, Dr. R. V.

Davie might be forgiven for taking a similar liberty with Mr. Ernest Stubbings. And there were the gulls to look at, and the boats, and the sea—particularly the sea.

He could hardly contain his impatience as he waited for the west-country train to leave Paddington.

FIVE

I

Rose Cottage is fifteen minutes' walk from the Ottery Arms, along the Exeter road and then down the hill on the right by the little common and the fir wood. Davie padded along in the face of the sun, carrying the snowstorm wrapped in a careful parcel.

He had known that high road before it was properly metalled, when every horse-drawn vehicle had gone past in a cloud of country dust, and when you might walk for twenty minutes and not even see a vehicle at all. The road was different now, but many of the houses were the same. In that garden on the right there was an enormous rhododendron. It had been there ever since Davie could remember. It was a deep rose colour and was always out a fortnight before any other rhododendron in Tidwell St. Peter's. And that house on the left, with the verandah and the cedars on the lawn, that was for ever associated in Davie's mind with lime juice. Davie's mother had not gone in for lime juice. But Mrs. Rotherham—that was the name—used to ask the children out to luncheon sometimes, and Mrs. Rotherham always had lime juice. She also took in the *Scout* magazine. As neither she nor Mr. Rotherham were scouts, Davie used to wonder why she got it. Only now did it occur to him, after about sixty years, that the good woman had almost certainly bought it in order to give it to him. Heavens, the kindnesses he had known once upon a time in Tidwell St. Peter's, in the longforgotten days when people had some money to do kindnesses with.

Another house, on the left, at the top of the hill, was approached by a long straight drive, lined with fir trees and rhododendrons. Davie had always been afraid of that house at the end of the vista. A lady had lived there whom nobody ever saw. She was an invalid, poor thing, but its unapproachability at the end of the drive had made the house seem sinister, and even today when the gates stood open, and two little boys were racing along the avenue on bicycles, shouting and ringing their bells, it still gave him a Bluebeard sort of feeling.

Nearly opposite this drive was the turning to Rose Cottage. Davie walked down the hill and presently stood before the gate, and, as on his previous visit, he waited a minute before going in, looking with pleasure at the roses rising behind the banks of lavender, and with criticism at the ugly gateposts. Red brick, old red brick, would have gone with Rose Cottage. Or wooden posts: that was what it would have had originally.

Then he opened the gate, walked up the incline, passed by a phalanx of fuchsias, and knocked on the open door.

"What ho!" said Mr. Parsley, "you've not been away long. Come in."

"I went away for a particular engagement," said Davie. "That over, something else fell through, and I thought I'd take the chance to come back. I want to finish at Cadleigh as soon as I can. So I'm back, and I thought I'd improve the occasion by bringing down my favourite snowstorm for you to see. It's curiously more appropriate than most of them. Look."

Davie unwrapped the parcel, and provoked the elements.

"You see, it's spring as we sometimes get it. A sheep and a lamb in a field, and the snow falling—but then the weather clears, and there they are in the meadow with the young flowers around them, and the background trees putting out their new leaves. I think it's pretty."

"Indeed it is. I've never seen one like it. May I?"

Arthur Parsley shook it again. "It's at its best when the snow is just clearing. The man who made that was a philosopher."

"Or wasn't," said Davie. "It is more likely he was just tired of making soup plates."

"Water is your need, I think," said Arthur Parsley. "I'll get some."

"Please. You are very kind."

The parlour and the kitchen were only separated by a door. Arthur Parsley turned the tap, and Davie could hear water splashing in the sink. Without hurrying, though his heart was thumping in his chest, he crossed the room to the shelf which held Parsley's collection of snowstorms, and picked up the cheap, modern dome, causing the snow, as he moved it, to stir lightly round the two boys playing guitars. Then, with an eye towards the door, he gave the base a firm turn counterclockwise. The thing unscrewed. He had expected that. Inside the base there was a sizable cavity, but it was empty and clean. Then he shook the top part and created the normal snowstorm. Clearly the detachable base and the performance in the dome were unconnected. Then, glancing again at the kitchen door, he screwed the base back, and set the boys on their shelf again.

He had completed the operation and turned away before Arthur Parsley came back with the water in one hand and a tin in the other.

"Nuts," said Mr. Parsley, "sorry to be so long. I was just opening a new tin."

"I behave badly with nuts," said Davie. "It has often been the subject of unfavourable comment."

But then the declining sun, suddenly unmasked, gleamed through the parlour window, illuminating the shelf of snowstorms with the precision of a search-light. It revealed that the flurry round the long-haired guitar players had not completely subsided.

"I see you've been at the Boys," said Arthur Parsley, handing Davie a glass.

"Yes, I did take that liberty. I wanted to see if the principle is the same. It seems to be. Where did you say you got it?"

"I don't think I did say," said Mr. Parsley. And instantly Davie wished he had shaped his question differently. It had been a leading question, the traditional trap. "Where did you get it?" would have been enough.

But Mr. Parsley was not hiding anything. "Rachel Merrick gave it to me," he said. "She saw it in Jane Gonzago's shop, and thought—how inaccurately!—that I would like it."

"I wonder where Jane Gonzago got it."

"You seem intrigued."

"Yes, I am. I've never seen a modern version."

"Probably she wouldn't remember. She's wonderfully vague. You know the shop? In Fore Street."

"Oh, *that*! It's a junk shop, isn't it?"

"Not entirely, but obviously, it's a hobby. I don't think she's poor. The shop's in one of those nice houses with a garden running up to the cliff, and the garden goes with the shop, which is very nice for her. That's how I got to know her; flowers—she knows about them."

"She actually lives in the end bit of Pinewood, I think."

"Yes."

"Gonzago—what an exquisite name! Is she the local representative of the Mafia?"

"Ha!" said Parsley. "You should see Jane Gonzago."

II

At that moment anyone might have seen Miss Gonzago. She was sitting in the little summer-house at the end of the garden running up to the cliff, drinking a late cup of tea, and staring out to sea. From time to time she surveyed the cliff path running to left and right below her wall, and as her observation post was perched some six feet above the path, it was possible for her to scrutinize the passers-by while they were at a distance, and yet to ignore them when they drew near. Straight over their heads she looked at the sparkling sea, and people rarely said, "Good evening, Miss Gonzago," because Miss Gonzago always looked so deeply engaged in the contemplation of infinity. Plain and thin, aged about fifty, invariably dressed many years behind the fashion, or indeed in no fashion at all, even given to the wearing of high collars and cameo brooches, Miss Gonzago was shy. But those who had got to know her liked her simple ways. She belonged to the Women's Institute. She won first prizes for quince jelly. She was secretary of the Horticultural Society. From time to time she did not scruple to offer her mild little voice to the alto section of the local choral society. Her Uncle Joseph, who had set her up in her antique shop, had been heard to say (but not before Miss Gonzago), "Jane's face is her fortune. She looks so innocent that people will think they're diddling her when really she'll be diddling them."

And Uncle Joseph had spoken shrewdly. Underneath her shyness there was strength in Miss Gonzago. As a child she had wanted to be a boy; as a girl she had wanted to be one of those intrepid women who cross the Sahara on a camel; and now, in middle age, such vigorous ambitions long abandoned, she had found a curious fulfilment of her earlier hopes in a business which for her was one long innocent excitement. She loved a bargain. She adored auctions. With the gentility of an Edwardian governess she occasionally participated in illegal "rings." Behind her back the other dealers called her Lady Golightly.

And so, this evening, there she was in her summer-house, sipping her tea, watching the gulls and the rowing boats, and, far out on the horizon, a yacht. Presently she picked up some letters from a weather-warped table beside her seat. Notices of auctions chiefly, a letter from a customer, a bill or two, a cheque, a letter from Uncle Joseph. She had read them already. Now she sorted them neatly on the table, and Uncle Joseph's letter she read a second time before tearing it up. Then she examined the sky.

There were no clouds at all. She felt sure it was set fair. And the day after tomorrow, that being Thursday, early closing day, on Thursday she would take her tea out on the beach.

It is impossible to walk far on the Tidwell St. Peter's beach. The stones will not accommodate you. You slide. You stumble. You are thankful to sit down. The average holiday-maker is lazy. He will go long distances by car, but he will not walk. A hundred yards on the Tidwell St. Peter's beach discourages the hardiest. Even in the best of weather the bathing beaches by the esplanade may be crowded and the whole of the rest of the great bay untenanted—because of the stones. It is, however, possible to walk along the cliff path and to get down to the beach at the Chine, which is a scramble nowadays, or further along, at the little sandy cove, which is practically a slide. Or there are other beaches which can be reached by boat. Miss Gonzago refused to slide, but she did not object to a scramble. She made mental arrangements to go to the Chine. Tomato sandwiches and hard-boiled eggs, thought Miss Gonzago, gazing out to sea with an expression of earnest compassion.

III

After dinner Davie telephoned to Irene. It was not an easy call to make. He had said he had finished in the library, and here he was back again. There had to be a reason, and it looked as if he might have to speak plainly. But Irene showed no surprise. Indeed she seemed pleased to hear his voice. "I'll ask Donald to pick you up—and you like nine thirty, don't you?"

"Yes, please."

"Nine thirty it is."

"Good night."

Irene was always brisk on the telephone. A rare and admirable quality in women.

Davie returned to the lounge, lowered himself into an armchair, and briefly reviewed his fellow visitors. Some were different from those of last week. Different but the same, so many white permanent waves, so many widows, so much cheerful conversation about the dead. "I haven't heard anything of Margaret for a long time." "Margaret died." "Did she? I didn't know." Rosemary had died too. Jean was not expected to last more than a week or so. It was, he supposed, a natural subject of conversation. The old ladies were glad to have beaten Margaret and Rosemary and Jean, but the race was not over.

Davie shut his eyes. It had been a long day. He hardly felt he could do any useful thinking. He felt sure that Arthur Parsley's snowstorm was a match with the snowstorm which ought to have been on K. W. Myrtle's mantelshelf. From the start he had asked himself why anyone should break into a college room and steal an inexpensive ornament, unless it had *contained* something. He hadn't the smallest doubt now that it *had* contained something—something in a cavity in its detachable base. "Snow" in a snowstorm! The cynicism was detestable.

The cavity in Arthur Parsley's snowstorm had been clean. Did he know it was there? Parsley had given nothing away. Was that because he had nothing to give away? Because he was not concerned? Possibly. But Davie had a distinct and uncomfortable feeling that Parsley had indeed noted his particular interest in the guitar players. That was bad luck. He had been betrayed by a sunbeam.

A gentle sleep descended on Dr. Davie. It was quite early when he awoke, barely half past ten, but the lounge was empty; the permanent waves had all retired.

Before retiring himself he walked up the garden to listen to those other waves, retiring and advancing, below the cliff. But it was low tide and a calm sea, the draw on the pebbles hardly audible.

SIX

I

"Let's go and sit in the rose garden," said Irene. "It's early, but there won't be any dew, not in this sun." So Irene wants to talk, thought Davie; otherwise she would have assumed that I needed to go to the library. He said, "Yes, indeed. Do let's do that." And Blanche, who had been standing irresolute on the terrace, also considered the idea, and decided to accompany them. The crane's-bill was the best place at high noon, but the rose garden made a pleasant change earlier in the day. She caught them up on the lower lawn and led the way to the rose garden steps, tail in air.

"You said you'd finished, R.V."

"I did. But I found some loose notes in the typescript, and now I must do some checking."

"Notes about what?"

"The last years."

"But the book stops in 1960. He wasn't adding anything, was he?"

"Not in that sense."

This is becoming sticky, thought Davie. But then Irene said, "Talking of notes—I hope you remembered to destroy that notebook, R.V." She had introduced the matter herself. That was a great relief.

"I wish you'd tell me, Irene, why you are so concerned about that notebook. The speculations in it are obscure to a point of perplexity. What are you worrying about?"

"You sound as if you haven't destroyed it, R.V. You promised you would."

"If you will tell me honestly why that notebook scares you, I will destroy it."

"It doesn't scare me."

"Yes, it does. The day I showed it to you you suddenly went pale. You were afraid of something."

"That was the day of the funeral. I was upset."

"There is something more, Irene, and I wish you'd tell me."

"I assure you, R.V.—"

"Then shall *I* tell *you*? You were worried because Donald was in Merrick's wood on the night that Merrick died."

Irene stared at him. He had not asked a question. Like some unwelcome crystal gazer he had stated a fact.

"How—"

"Robert told me."

"*Robert!*"

"In his notes. Robert also told me that Donald telephoned to you that night to tell you Merrick was dead. Naturally, Robert wondered how Donald could know so quickly. Naturally he remembered that Donald had been in the wood. Naturally these things upset him. You could have explained to him."

"No."

"Only because you were afraid of involving Donald. You would have had to admit that he was in the wood that evening, and that you knew it. You would have had to remember why he was in the wood. Irene, if you had to tell a jury these things, you might be afraid. There is no reason to be afraid of me."

"How much did Robert—think he knew?"

"That I can't say. But he knew you were in trouble. And he presumed that Donald was acting on your behalf. What else could he presume? Was it true?"

And as Irene did not answer, he went on, "I will tell you a secret, Irene; and, if this conversation is to be continued, I've got to tell you a secret. There really is some doubt whether Adam Merrick died in an accident."

He waited, but she said nothing.

"I think you trust Donald. You do not believe that he could have had anything to do with the matter."

"Of course he hadn't."

"But you are determined not to discuss it because an explanation will disclose some secret in your own life. Some secret that you wanted to keep from Robert. You should understand that the clearing up of a murder is more important than the protection of your secrets. If you tell me the truth you may help the investigation, and not necessarily expose your troubles at all. If you don't tell me the truth, and this enquiry has to be completed without your help, you might find that your secrets are accidentally exposed anyhow."

He looked at her, asking her to speak, but Irene did not answer. He waited, and while he waited he contemplated the beautiful Blanche, outstretched upon the flagstones. She matched with everything. Then he looked across the roses to the faun in the eastern apse of the garden. The sun had just mounted above the yew hedge and touched him on the shoulder. Then he looked back to Irene, sitting beside him on the teak garden bench.

"Irene."

Still she did not speak.

"Irene. Please talk. What does it matter now? Whatever it was is over."

"It is not over, R.V. Not until Adam Merrick's death is explained."

It was Davie's turn to be surprised.

"So—you had doubts about it, too."

"Of course I had. Who wouldn't have? That night Adam Merrick had told me to meet him in the wood. Donald wouldn't let me. He said he'd have it out with him. Adam Merrick died. Until there's proof there's always suspicion. You can trust someone totally—and yet, and yet, because of something unexplained, there remains a veil between you. Of course I don't believe that Donald had anything to do with it, but I want it proved that somebody else had."

"Hadn't you better begin at the beginning?"

"Yes. I don't mind now I've started. Donald and I met in London two years before I married Robert. We were third cousins, but we'd never known each other before. We became lovers—lovers who quarrelled and made it up, and quarrelled and made it up, and one day answered an advertisement for a cruise in a yacht called *Rachel*, belonging to a Mr. Adam Merrick. It was a disaster. Mrs. Merrick was on the cruise, and she took a fancy for Donald, and what Rachel Merrick takes a fancy for Rachel Merrick gets. I was miserable. Donald was miserable too, really. Of course we quarrelled. The final bust up

took place in Portoferraio. I went off to dine by
myself that night—and that was how I met Robert.
In the mood I was in I was ready for anything. It
doesn't seem reasonable that I should have had such
wonderful good fortune. Robert was the most aston-
ishing person."

"He was."

"He had the heart of a man of forty, the charm of
a man of thirty. At that moment he was the only
man for me. I fell for him absolutely."

"He fell for you."

"Going round the world with Robert was pure
joy. He was the most interesting, well-informed, amus-
ing, kindest man I ever met—but—"

"But?"

"He was seventy. And sometimes I used to think of
Donald, and wish we'd never quarrelled—wish I could
have both of them. It sounds awful. I don't want
to be awful, R.V."

"You're not awful, Irene. Just honest."

"When we got back to London our return was mentioned in the papers. You know those ghastly familiar
paragraphs in the gossip column."

"Full well I do."

"One of them mentioned our hotel, and one afternoon when Robert was out, Donald called. I can't
expect you to sympathize. I loved Robert. I did love
Robert, R.V. But I loved Donald too. It sounds mad,
dishonourable, unjust, greedy—but I agreed to de-
ceive Robert. Donald wanted to write. He wanted to
be where we could meet. I asked Robert to let him
live at the lodge and be our chauffeur. And of course
we did meet."

It was like the end of a chapter. Irene bent down

and tweaked a wild pansy from between two flagstones. For some seconds she sat there twirling it
about in her fingers. Then she threw it away and
the flower fell beside Blanche, and seemed appropriate there. Love-in-idleness: Blanche goes with everything, Davie repeated to himself.

"Our happiness ended three weeks after we'd got
home. Someone came to call, and mentioned that
Pinewood had been taken by people called Merrick—
Adam Merrick. Whether it was a coincidence, or
whether he knew about it I don't know, but as soon
as Adam Merrick got back from that cruise he had
settled down in Tidwell St. Peter's. And, not long
after I heard he was there, he got in touch with me.
It was the finest opportunity for blackmail that anybody ever had. He used it. That's all there is to
say. Now do you understand why I am nervous about
anything connected with him? It was a relief when
he died—but new worries followed. How had he died?
Why had he died? And then Robert began to take
an interest in the case."

"So the blue notebook wasn't a surprise?"

"No. He got an idea that there was something
wrong. I couldn't be sure what it was that he suspected. Guiltily I was afraid he suspected me. And
if he suspected not me but Donald—that was worse,
because that would mean he had found a reason to
suspect him."

"And he had some reason, hadn't he? He saw him
go to Merrick's wood. He heard him ring you up and
tell you that Merrick was dead. How do you explain
that?"

"I don't, R.V. You must ask Donald. I'm glad you
got me to talk, but I've said as much as I can."

"Your interests and mine are identical in this matter, Irene. If I may I'll go and find Donald."

"He'll be at the Lodge. He's driving me to Exeter at twelve, so—"

"So goodbye, and thank you for your confidence."

Turning back at the steps to wave a hand he saw that Irene was sitting up straight on the bench, looking down towards the lake. She had the same expression of relief on her face as she had had that day when she returned the notebook, glad because of its obscurity and insufficiency. She was an odd girl, thought Davie. And then Blanche, seeing him hesitate, was reminded how much she enjoyed a short walk with a gentleman; and she arose and followed him in a stately and deliberate manner. Davie waited for her and stroked her as she passed him by, for Blanche liked to lead the way when walking with friends.

"What now, Beautiful?" said Davie when they reached the terrace. Blanche rolled on her back.

"And a very good idea," said Davie. "But it's a little early for me. And I'm afraid I have things to do. Goodbye."

Blanche made no answer to that. She had already purred herself into a doze.

II

Davie walked two hundred yards down the drive till he reached the beginning of the lime tree avenue, and there he turned to the right, down the lesser drive, between the rhododendrons, sombre now that

their season of flowers was past. From there it was
only five minutes walk to Donald's cottage orné.

In the days of the Sir Robert who built it, the
lodgekeeper had needed to look both ways to supply
an immaculate service. One window looks towards
the gates, and one looks back along the drive. It was
in the window that looks along the drive that Donald kept his writing table. As he approached, Davie
could see him standing there, back to the window.
He was in the act of cradling the telephone, the private line between the lodge and the house. So Irene
had been talking to him. It was natural enough that
she should, and yet it lent an air of conspiracy to
the little house. He would have been better pleased
to be unannounced.

Donald heard him coming up the path, and opened
the door.

"Come in."

"I'm sorry to interrupt your labours," said Davie
"—at least I hope I am interrupting. I trust you
weren't reading the papers or listening to the wireless
on this fine working day."

Donald said, "Will you sit here?" Evidently he was
not for joking.

"I have been talking to Irene," Davie went on,
"and there came a point in our conversation when
she said I'd better talk to you, and I think so too—
so please, Donald, may I?"

He had gone straight to the point on purpose. Donald had certainly been warned about what he was
going to ask. The less negotiations the better.

"What's the trouble?" said Donald.

He's wary, thought Davie. If he's got anything to
hide I shan't get much out of him. But if he hasn't

he'll say something useful. He *must* say something useful. Why did he know about Merrick's death so soon?

"Donald, I won't go into it at length, but I've been troubled to find that Robert did have serious doubts about the death of Adam Merrick. You remember that notebook?"

"Yes."

"Since then I've found other notes."

In any narrative the moment of discovery is dramatic. The listener takes a quick breath, opens his eyes wide, grips the side of his chair. He has been surprised. Donald was not surprised. "Irene looked for them," he said. "But she couldn't find a thing."

"You *expected* there were notes?"

It was Davie who had to sound surprised.

"Yes. Robert had got interested, suspicious, in the end seriously involved. Adam Merrick occupied his mind—and his mind was something he liked to put on paper. We were sure there were notes somewhere. What did he say?"

"He said he'd seen you go into the wood that night. He said he'd heard you telephone to Irene to tell her that Merrick was dead. It was apparently remarkably soon after he had been found by Giles Gifford and Jason. Naturally Robert was interested. Naturally he was troubled. Now that you realize that I know as much as I do—will you tell me the rest? It will help me. It ought not to harm you."

"I don't know why you can't let well alone."

"There are reasons."

"I wouldn't have told you four months ago—but, all right, I will now."

"Thank you."

"You already know why I was in the wood. I was there to find Adam Merrick. He thought he was going to meet Irene. I wouldn't let her go. Adam Merrick was blackmailing her. There are legal ways of dealing with blackmailers, but they are difficult ways. Robert would have found out, and Irene was terrified of that. She did love Robert."

"I know she did."

"A better way of dealing with a blackmailer is to knock his block off. I was prepared to do that. He wouldn't have complained. I knew too much about him.

"It was dusk when I got among the pine trees behind the quarry. That was where the meeting was to be. I waited. He was late. Then I heard the clink of the little iron wicket gate down by the brook. It's the back gate of the Merrick property, and the gate to the public path."

Davie nodded. He knew where everything was in Tidwell St. Peter's.

"That surprised me. I thought he'd be coming from the house. But if he were coming from the road, that would explain why he was late. He'd been detained somewhere. So then I waited for his steps up the path—but they didn't come. I couldn't understand that. He wouldn't *not* come. And then I heard something which took me entirely by surprise. I heard the sound of the wicket gate again—the lifted latch and then the clink as it swung back into place. That meant one of of two things: either the person who had come in had gone out again, or a second person had come in. I waited a bit longer, and then I did hear steps coming up the path. And then there was a sort of a thud, and a cry, and then, after a moment's silence, a distant splash. Of course I knew what had happened. Someone had fallen into the quarry.

"I couldn't see anyone else, but it was dark among the trees. I got to the edge of the quarry and peered over. I couldn't see anything. But I could see people in the road, just passers-by, I think, who'd chosen that time of all times to stop for a chat. I couldn't run down the path and out by the gate. If I'd been recognized I'd have been in a terrible position afterwards. They moved on, but by then I'd got scared. There might be someone else passing by. I couldn't get myself to go down, but I was horrified to think that there might be someone wanting my help."

"Even if he were Adam Merrick?" said Davie.

"Yes. I said I'd knock his block off. Strangely enough that doesn't mean killing."

Davie nodded. The oddities of idiom were always delightful to him.

"And then I heard voices in the wood, and naturally I stayed hidden. And then I heard voices in the quarry. I crept back to the edge. I could see two men with torches. I heard Giles Gifford say, 'He's here, Basil.' So I knew who they were. Then I saw them fish him out, and I heard Giles say, 'He's dead.' And then I belted off the way I'd come—to the other side of the pine wood, across the road, and back through Cadleigh woods."

"But how did you know that it was Adam Merrick?" asked Davie.

For a moment Donald seemed stuck for an answer. Then, "It had to be Merrick," he said. "Who else could it be, with Basil Jason looking for him?"

"When you spoke on the telephone," said Davie,

"you spoke as though Irene must know what you were talking about—*whom* you were talking about."

"I think she did know. What else had she been thinking about all day? When she heard my voice she expected me to speak about Adam Merrick."

"That was one of the things that worried Robert. He knew you were in the wood. He heard what you said to Irene. She seemed to understand what you said without explanation."

"I think that makes sense, Dr. Davie."

To himself Davie said "H'm," but added "And yet perhaps it does." To Donald he said, "Is there anything else you know about Merrick?"

"He was a rogue. In the Mediterranean I'm pretty sure he smuggled."

"Smuggled what?"

"Dope."

"What about here, in England?"

"I don't know. I wouldn't be surprised. Why are you so interested?"

"Because I smell a motive. If I were looking for a reason for killing this unpleasant little man with his evil temper and his delight in flowers—like Goering drooling over his looted pictures—I would say that blackmail might have prompted two—no, three— possible killers, hatred two other ones, and professional rivalry a sixth."

"Professional rivalry?"

"Yes. Nothing promotes death so well as a feud between villains. Have you anything else to tell me?"

"Not a thing," said Donald Bride.

III

Donald had offered to drive him back, but Davie had preferred to walk. It was only eleven o'clock. It would be good for the liver. And good for other reasons. He did not want to go on talking with Donald Bride, not just at present.

When he reached the shops it was a little after half past eleven. High Street was full of cars, the pavements full of people, bobbing in and out of shops, chatting in the middle of the sidewalk, and particularly sneaking in and out of Turpin's or Wonnacott's for that mid-morning cup of coffee with cream cakes which has hastened so many old ladies on the path to glory. The very old ladies wore gay little straw hats with bunches of flowers perched on the brim; the very old gentlemen wore a covering of some sort; but the under-seventies, Davie noticed, had hardly a hat among them. What had happened to the trade, he wondered. One still saw hats in the windows, but who bought them? That was an enquiry ripe for neglect by the social historian.

He went on down the street, looking at the shops, and wishing all the time that people were not so fond of destroying and altering. He could remember when most of these houses had had thatched roofs. That had been changed long ago, and might have been necessary as a fire precaution. But there had been no wisdom at all in pulling the shop fronts about. Those chromium letters did not promise greater quality. The old small windows enticed the passerby with the suggestion of hidden joys within. The great wide windows repelled with their suggestion that here was the lot; if you didn't see what you wanted, then you could be sure they hadn't got it.

Davie went on down Fore Street, where the brook so delightfully emerges from beneath the houses, and babbles along beside the street towards the sea. Presently he came to a stand before Miss Gonzago's window. There are some very good antique shops in Tidwell St. Peter's. Jane Gonzago's place was more of a curio shop. There was a pretty tea pot standing between a stuffed ferret and a bead footstool. There were books as well as Staffordshire figures. Through the window he could see Miss Gonzago attending to a lady customer. Her rather large hands fluttered around vaguely and finally alighted on a luster milk jug. With an air of gentle resignation she held it up for inspection. Davie suddenly got a feeling that he would like to see Miss Gonzago leading the altos in "Go up, go up, thou Baldhead!"

Pleased with that speculation he passed on down the street, rounded the old stone wall at the beginning of the esplanade, and made his way back up the cliff path towards the garden of the Ottery Arms. But before going in he sat down on a public bench. At the other end of the bench was a weather-beaten old cove in a reefer jacket, his blue eyes solemnly watching the sea as though it were his book. Davie was quickly in conversation.

"There doesn't seem to be any mackerel fishing nowadays."

"All over," said the old cove.

"When I was a boy the fishermen used to sit up here and watch the sea for the shoals, and suddenly one of them would cry out and point at a glittering in the water, and they'd all rush down to the beach and jump into a boat and row out in a circle, paying out a net. It would be quite close to shore."

"So it were."

"And then they'd land and draw in the net and the children would help pull."

"So they did," said the old cove.

"I used to pull," said Davie.

"Did you, then?"

"And when the haul was landed we used to be given a fish for our services. I fear it must have been a gross overpayment."

"It's all finished now," said the old cove. "The mackerel boats is all over to Exmouth."

"That's sad."

"Well, there's crabs and lobsters. Walter Ford, now, he's lobsters. That's him, mister, down there on the beach looking after his lobster pots. When I was young they got all the lobsters they wanted with a rowing boat in the cove t'other side of the rocks, but nowadays with they new-fangled motorboats they go miles for 'em. And they ain't no better than they used to be, neither."

For a few moments the old cove fell silent, gazing across the bay, thinking, perhaps, of old days with the mackerel nets. Davie took the opportunity to glance down at Mr. Ford. He was sitting on an upturned box on the beach, just below Miss Gonzago's garden wall. It was his pitch. Walter Ford was small and dark, and, in the manner of an earlier age, he actually wore little gold rings in his ears. If he had claimed to be the original sailor in Ambrose Faddle's masterpiece, the visitors would hardly have disbe-

lieved him, and in fact his great-grandfather had been
the very man. Davie could remember the Ford family
when he was a child. They had always looked as if
they were bound for Rio.

"Me," said the old cove suddenly reclaiming attention, "I took up with gardening. There's always work
for a gardener in this place, though some don't know
any more about gardening than my backside. But I'd
always had my bit of garden, and I knew, you see.
Of course I was in the Navy in the war, back in
1918, and losted two of my fingers—in a accident
that were—" he said, with a touch of pride, "but it
don't make no difference, and I've been doing gardening for thirty years now. I used to do four gardens, but it's too much now, with my back. You have
to ease off as you grow older, mister, as I expect you've
found out, so now I only does Mr. Stubbings, Mon-
day and Thursday, and the rest of the time I comes
up yer and looks at the sea."

"Then you must be Mr. Challice," said Davie with
sudden respect.

"Aye—I'm Challice. Did you yer of me, mister?"

"Yes indeed. Someone told me you were a good
gardener."

"Aye," said Mr. Challice complacently.

"Didn't you make Mr. Stubbings's water garden?"

"Aye. I was working in that there very garden, mister, on the evening when Mr. Merrick went and fell
over the quarry after having high words with Mr.
Stubbings. You yerd about that, I expect?"

"Not very much. I wasn't here at the time. What
happened?"

"Well it were like this yer, mister—"

And so Davie was regaled with the Challice legend,

performed by the master himself, and "That's an interesting story," he said at the conclusion.

"It were a proper old caper," said Mr. Challice.

"And it was shortly after that, on his way home, that Mr. Merrick slipped over the quarry?"

"Aye," said Mr. Challice, adding darkly, "so they say. It were a funny way to go home, up by the path round the quarry."

"Was there no one else about? No one who might have seen what happened?"

"Nobody strange, mister. I see Mrs. Merrick down in the daffodils, just before I left, but it were getting dark. She would have been going home—the proper way. And when I come out of the back gate, I see Miss Gonzago out for a stroll. She were standing by the hedge, listening to those two quarrelling, like I were, but when she see me coming up the hill, she give up, lady-like, and comes on down the road and says 'Good evening, Mr. Challice,' and I says 'Good evening, Miss Gonzago,' and neither of us said a word about they two arguing. It wouldn't have been nice."

"No," said Davie. "I can see that. It wouldn't. You were quite right."

"Aye. So there we all were, going away from the quarry just before Mr. Merrick fell over it, mister. And that's all I know about it."

It wasn't much, but it was a little more than he had learnt from Giles, thought Davie as he walked down the garden path towards the Ottery and refreshment.

IV

Although Davie was a great man for an afternoon doze, he was wakeful when his heart and mind were joined in an adventure. Today he closed his eyes for not more than fifteen minutes after luncheon. He sat still for another fifteen minutes turning over in his mind certain fragments of information, and then he arose, collected his binoculars, and set off for a walk. Crossing the village street opposite the hotel, he climbed the hill towards Pinewood, passed the gates, turned left, and so, by a leafy lane that skirted the Merrick woods, he found the road where Giles had brought him the day they had visited the quarry. He wanted to take another look at the place on his own.

It was quiet on the floor of the old quarry. The water in the pool was already lower. The umbrella spokes stuck a little further into the air. The boot had positively come to land. A bird made a sudden fuss in one of the young oak trees, and flew away. The silence became complete.

Playing at scouting games with Robert, Davie remembered being scared in this quiet place. Even now he felt that old sensation, the cold finger on the spine. He gave a little shudder and decided to move upward into the sun.

A third of the way up he found an elder bush. It was good cover, and there was no difficulty in looking between its branches. He stood behind it and took out his binoculars. First he took a look at Rose

Cottage. Arthur Parsley was on his knees diligently planting out chrysanthemums. Then he looked to the left, and observed the storks and windmills, the bridges and pagodas of Mr. Stubbings's absurd water garden. Further up the denuded slope the colours clashed in Mr. Stubbings's geometrical flower beds. A little higher there were shrubs, and finally, between the shrubs, Mr. Stubbings himself, on the verandah in a deck chair, his binoculars beside him on a garden table.

The binoculars—there they were again. Was Mr. Stubbings just curious? The aboriginal prodnose, as Giles had called him. Was he a bird watcher? Or had the quarry some fascination for him? Had he some need to keep an eye on it? These are not facts, Davie told himself; don't imagine things. He studied Mr. Stubbings and decided that he was asleep. It was an opportunity not to be missed. He moved on up the incline, and after twenty paces stubbed his toe on a stone and fell flat on his face. This time there was no Giles to catch him.

"Damn and blast," said Davie out loud. "Stones have no right among bracken; they don't belong there." He screwed himself into a sitting position, poked around with his hand, and presently disturbed a round flat stone the size of an open hand. "Well, I'm damned," he muttered. "A beach stone. That has even less right." He turned it about, and was suddenly interested. It was a beach stone, but not from the beach. Originally from the beach, of course, but not recently from the beach. Across the diameter of the stone was a girdle of mortar. Anyone could see that this was a stone that had at some time been mortared into a wall. Now why, he asked himself, would anyone remove such a stone, and why would anyone drop it here? At any other time the question might have seemed unprofitable, but today it reminded him of his talk about beach stones with Mrs. Merrick, and of the beach stone in the picture of the front door at Pinewood. And that brought Adam Merrick into his mind—short, dark, dapper and dead. And then he noticed, firmly wedged into a crack in the mortar, three hairs. They were black hairs.

Davie put the stone down again among the bracken and sat quite still. Suddenly he felt too excited to move. Thoughts were racing through his head. A stone—a stone that crashed against the head of a man —a man who staggered to the edge of the quarry and fell over into the water—near enough to a boulder which could have done the damage, which was believed to have done the damage. Did someone have a brilliantly good idea? To fell a man with a stone and afterwards collect that stone and put it back where it came from? It would be a fine thing to have the evidence against you neatly mortared into a wall, or looking as though it were. Well, why didn't the person do it? Perhaps he, or she, couldn't find it. The person could hardly display himself searching for something in the darkness with a torch. And the following day the police would be on duty. Later, when a search might have been possible, it would have seemed no longer necessary. The authorities had decided for accidental death. In which case, if you had the nerve, far better to leave it where it was. Far better never to go near the place again. That might have been the sequence of decisions, each one agonizingly important. And yes, said Davie to his heart, I didn't really believe in all this till now. But here is a weapon that might positively be proved to be a murder weapon. Guess work? Presumption? There is no presumption or guess work about those hairs. They are human hairs, black hairs. A pathologist would have no difficulty in showing them to be Merrick's hairs—if they *are* Merrick's hairs.

So what was to be done? He had to secure the stone, but he did not want to walk through the street carrying it in his hand. It was too big for his pocket. Besides, it must not be rubbed. He would have to return with a carrier bag. And now he must hide it—hide it somewhere lower down. Up here he was more in the field of Mr. Stubbings's questing binoculars. Had that dismal man some inward compulsion to watch this area? It was a theory that sprang too easily to the mind. One didn't know.

One didn't know.

Davie did not know, for instance, that he was within much closer observation of a man who was standing on the footpath only a few paces away, and a little above him. The air had contained only the scents of summer. But now he became aware of the additional smell of Turkish tobacco. He looked up over his shoulder.

"Afternoon," said the man.

"Good afternoon."

"You're not very wise, if I may say so, sunning yourself so near the edge of a precipice. All you've got to do is to nod off—"

"I wasn't nodding off," said Davie. "I was indulging in a reverie."

"About quarries?"

"No—about Man."

"A proper study," said the man drily, "but more safely conducted somewhere else."

"You're quite right sir," said Davie, heaving himself on to his feet.

"I believe I've seen you in the village, or on the cliff—somewhere, I'm sure. My name is Basil Jason," said the man.

"Mine is Davie," said Davie, brushing a few scraps of grass from his trousers. "I expect you live here," he added, as innocently as though he had never heard the name of Jason outside the pages of Greek mythology. "I don't, but I used to, years ago. I like poking around and looking at old haunts. I remember this place when it was in working order."

"Well, don't fall over it—that's all I say. Someone did, not long ago. It ought to be railed—bits of it are. Actually you're trespassing."

"I suppose I am—but not, I hope, on your property."

"No."

"I take it, it belongs to Mrs. Merrick."

"Yes, it does."

"I know Mrs. Merrick. I don't think she'd mind." Mr. Jason looked interested.

"Didn't you go over the house the other day?"

"Yes."

"Are you going to take it?"

"I'm not sure."

"Well, don't miss it for want of making up your mind. A lot of other people have been over it."

Mr. Jason did not explain how he came to know so much about Mrs. Merrick's business.

"I must examine my purse," said Davie. "Goodbye," he added with an amiable smile. He was adopting the same maneuver that Giles had used on Mr. Stubbings, and it earned the same dividend.

"Goodbye," said Basil Jason, after a moment's hesitation. Then he passed on up the path to the wood, leaving behind him the faint savour of the Turkish cigarette. It made Davie think of Cambridge in the twenties. He had smoked then. Lovely great fat cigarettes called Weinbergers . . . That occupied his head for precisely two seconds. Then he was asking himself how long the man had been there. Davie had been sitting, staring at the bracken for some minutes, and he had put the stone down as soon as he recognized its importance—put it down to avoid disturbing it in any way. There was, he thought, a fair chance that Jason had not been watching him long. Davie had only noticed the cigarette a second before the man spoke. But it was more than ever essential to hide the stone in a different place.

He picked up a stick and pushed it into the ground to mark the place where the stone had lain. It would be important to be right about that. Then he picked up the stone and walked carefully down the incline to the gravel pit. Over to the left, near the padlocked shed, there was a crowd of nettles in a corner and behind them a mass of purple willow herb. He put it among the willow herb to save his fingers. He was screened by trees and bushes from the road and windows. There was no one standing on the quarry's edge. Unless someone were positively spying on him, the stone would be safe there.

Then he walked out into the road, and went downhill to the brook, and up the hill on the other side past Arthur Parsley's rose-decked cottage, and so out on to the high road.

On the way home he considered Mr. Jason. Tall, dark, good-looking in a spivvy way, he was too elegantly dressed for country walking. Giles had said the man was a traveller in cosmetics. That seemed odd. Everyone knows that cosmetics are overpriced, but it is the makers who earn the profits, not the reps. He thought Mr. Jason must represent other things besides cosmetics. All things considered, he was against Mrs. Merrick's lover.

V

It was teatime when he got back to the Ottery. And as another Devonian postponed the armada till his convenience, so Davie thought tea and a rest were more important than bustling back to the field. Indeed, he was tired; he needed his cup of tea. And when he had finished he felt in his pocket for the blue notebook. Except for the first four pages it was empty. He wanted to set down the thoughts that were chasing around in his head.

ADAM MERRICK (he wrote) died, I now think, from a blow on the back of the head and subsequent suffocation in the water of the pool in the gravel pit. I may have found the weapon. There are hairs on it which would clinch that matter. Anyone could have thrown the stone, but the fact that it was taken from a wall suggests deliberation. Someone must have known it was there, loose, and ready to take. And somewhere there is either a wall with a gap, or else a gap which has been filled in by something which does not really belong there. To spot that would be a little easier than looking for a particular stone on the beach, but not much.

It is too late now to be really certain about people. I can only make notes about the people who are known to have been in the vicinity. They are a curious lot.

First there is STUBBINGS, angry, as a man usually is when he is on the wrong side in a quarrel, and his grand position in Tidwell St. Peter's suddenly threatened. Merrick, it seems, was in a position to expose him. In some men that would certainly be a good reason for instant action. The gardens on West Hill were created in the grand manner. I don't think there are any beach stone boundaries up there. Stubbings could have followed Merrick down the hill. Somebody did, according to Arthur Parsley.

Secondly, there is RACHEL MERRICK and—I may as well link them—BASIL JASON. We know Jason was out because Giles says he was late for his drinks appointment. We know Mrs. Merrick was out because Challice saw her. They are lovers. Lovers have done abominable things to husbands before now. She had a beach stone by her door, but it was not this one. I don't think Pinewood has a beach-stone wall. But if someone did take a stone from a wall it doesn't follow that it was from their own wall. They'd be more clever if they took one from somebody else's.

Thirdly, there are IRENE and DONALD BRIDE. Irene was certainly being blackmailed by Merrick. It is difficult to think that she had anything to do with this. But Donald might have done it. He was there. According to his own account he intended to have it out with Merrick. The rest of his story is an unsupported alibi—"elsewhere" by about fifty yards. And it is exactly the sort of story that a liar might make up.

Fourthly, I have to dare to add ROBERT. He was there. But the notes that he wrote are bewildered. He was anxious for Irene, but he did not know what was wrong. It is a pity that he was going to West Tidwell that night. That took him past the quarry. His normal way home would have been up the hill and turn right, not down the hill to the brook.

Davie drew a line. Then underneath it he wrote.

Also present, ARTHUR PARSLEY, CHALLICE and MISS GONZAGO. One could no doubt imagine motives for any of them, but not with honesty, not with the facts that I have.

Old Challice said that "everyone" was going away from the quarry, but that is nonsense. It just made a dramatic end to his story. *He* was going away. He did not know which way Mrs. Merrick was going. And Miss Gonzago was actually going towards the quarry. She had to reach it before she would be going away from it. And perhaps she did not reach it. If Miss Gonzago were going home the quickest way, she would have gone through the gate to the public path

and the path through the daffodils to Pinewood
—the gate that Merrick would soon be using on
leaving Quarry View. In that event she would
have been close on Rachel Merrick's heels; and,
had she happened to linger, not far from the
subsequent tragedy. If, on the other hand, Miss
G. were going home by the leafy lane beyond
the quarry, to the right, she would not have been
anywhere near the public path at the crucial
time.

As evidence Challice's talk is muddled. But
without him we should not know that those two
women were so handy. Too handy perhaps. They
could not have known that Merrick was going
to be delayed by Stubbings.

Then he drew another line and, after a minute's
thought, he wrote,

Obviously this investigation would be advanced
if one could establish the place where that stone
came from.

Then he drew another line, closed the notebook, put
it in his pocket, leant back in his chair, and closed
his eyes. He drifted into a pleasant doze. Davie could
do that almost as easily as the beautiful Blanche.

In a far corner of the lounge Mrs. Watchett lifted
her gaze from the pages of her novel and looked across
the room over the top of her spectacles. Mrs. Watchett lived in the hotel. She read a novel a day, and
was the leading obituarist among the permanent
waves. It was she who had known what had happened
to Margaret. Mrs. Watchett had just finished her tea

when Davie came in, and she recognized him immediately: the old gentleman who had behaved so oddly
a few afternoons back, when she had been in the
lounge alone. Sitting there, furrowing his forehead,
scribbling in his notebook, he was, she feared, a little
mad. And now he had gone to sleep, and the next
thing, she supposed, would be that he'd sit up and
say "Of course" in a loud voice.

But the next thing was that young Giles Gifford
came into the room and went up to the old gentleman, who opened his eyes instantly and began to
talk just as though he hadn't been to sleep at all.
Mrs. Watchett did not choose to stare and unfortunately at that distance she could not hear. It was
vexing. She was obliged to return to her novel.

"Hullo, Giles."

"I heard you were back."

"Did you, indeed? Someone must be short of news."

"It was Arthur Parsley. He said he saw you out
for a walk this afternoon."

"Ah yes, I did go past his house." (He very much
hoped Parsley had not seen him in the quarry.)

"How is it you're back so soon, Dr. Davie?" Giles
cast a precautionary glance round the room. There
was no one in sight but Mrs. Watchett. "Any news,
sir?"

"Perhaps, Giles. Have you got your car?"

"Yes."

"Have you perchance a carrier bag, or, better, a
small rigid basket with a bit of clean paper at the
bottom?"

"Yes. There's a basket with a lot of muck in it.
I could heave that out."

"And clean paper?"

"There are some groceries in a lot of unnecessary bags. I can pinch one of those."

"Good. Shall we go then?"

"Certainly." The boldness, the obscurity of Dr. Davie's directions excited him greatly. "Where to, sir?"

"To the quarry, Giles," said Davie, hauling himself out of his chair.

Over the top of her glasses Mrs. Watchett marked their departure. A very odd pair she thought they were. She must ask Bea Wimbush about them. Bea made it a point of pride to know all about everybody.

Two hours had gone by since Davie hid the stone among the willow herb. The sun now shone on Mr. Stubbings's garden and on the roses that clambered about Rose Cottage. But the quarry was in shadow. It was very quiet. No bird sang.

"Let's be quick," said Davie. "It's over there in the corner. You've got the basket?"

On their earlier visit Davie and Giles had walked up the eastern curve of the quarry. The nettles and the willow herb were on the opposite side. It was only fifty paces from the entrance.

"It's in there," said Davie.

Giles bent down and parted the purple flowers.

"I don't see a stone," he said.

"Let me look," said Davie. "I know exactly where it is." Crouching down, for a moment suddenly anxious, he reached his hand under the leaves. But the stone was there. He drew it out and placed it in Giles's basket on top of a paper bag bearing the legend "Pearcey's Stores, The Best in Devon." In these days, thought Davie, when every shop sells exactly the same branded goods, the claim was extravagant. He could remember when old Mrs. Pearcey presided over that emporium and sold live crabs on the one hand and liquid blacking on the other. It was a solemn thought. Liquid blacking had been part of the nineteenth century. No one was ever going to see it again.

"And this one can go on top," said Giles. Unabashed, on a second bag, Pearcey's Stores reiterated its claim to primacy.

"Come on," said Davie.

They turned about and walked towards the entry.

The young oaks and the great chunk of bramble masked them from the road. They also masked Mr. Stubbings, who stood by the entrance peering into the quarry. Giles saw him first. He laid a hand on Davie's sleeve.

They waited behind the mass of bramble, while Mr. Stubbings, on the other side, advanced into the quarry and looked about him cautiously.

"What the hell does *he* want?" whispered Giles.

"Us," said Davie. "He must have seen us come in. He wants to know why."

"I'm not so sure of that," said Giles. "We didn't go up the slope. I doubt if he can see much of the floor of the quarry from his place—not with all this greenery. He doesn't look as though he were hunting any one. He looks as though he wanted to be sure he wasn't being watched himself."

Mr. Stubbings had now reached the shed. He was examining the door, scrutinizing the ground in front of the door, peering at the path.

"He's looking to see if anyone's been meddling with

the shed," said Davie. "He may be on his rights as chairman of the council."

"If it wasn't so dry we could have given him some footprints."

"I don't think I want to run into him," said Davie. "We can get out now. Come on."

Two minutes later they were climbing into the car. Then they drove slowly down the hill, over the brook, and up the hill on the other side. It was the second time that afternoon that Davie had passed Rose Cottage.

This time Arthur Parsley was standing by his gate, trimming the hedge. Giles lifted his hand to smack out a honk of greeting on the horn, and then restrained himself.

"Better not," he said.

"Much better not," said Davie. "But I'm glad we saw him. I am suddenly reminded of something I had forgotten, or, rather, of something I had not thought essential to remember."

Giles gave him a sidelong look. "Not his telephone number?" he said.

"No," said Davie. "Not that at all."

At the bottom of West Hill, a little before the shops begin, Giles glanced at his passenger again. He was looking ahead but not at the passing scene. He was clearly engaged on some private speculation of his own, and what he saw provoked a faint smile round the corners of his mouth and a brightness in his grey-green eyes.

Giles swept the aged motor up to the steps of the Ottery. But Davie did not immediately open the door.

He said, "Giles—"

"Yes?"

"I have something revolving in my mind which may be a bit of wrong-headed guess work. I must think about it a bit more. But if it isn't—"

"Yes?"

"What are you doing tomorrow night?"

"I'm supposed to be going to a dinner party. It wouldn't be easy—"

"You *are* going to a dinner party. You'll be leaving when?"

"A little before eleven, normally, but I might contrive—"

"Contrive nothing. Could you be here at twelve o'clock?"

"Of course."

"Then please do that. If I decide I'm justified, I want to take a small liberty with somebody else's property. And I'd rather not do it alone."

"I'll come."

"Good—but not to the hotel, and don't be earlier than twelve. I'll be in the street. Just cruise along and pick me up."

"Pointing which way?"

"We'll begin by going along the West Tidwell Road."

"Right. Can you get out?"

"No, I can't. Just give me a shove. Thanks. See you tomorrow, unless I telephone."

"On the dot," said Giles.

VI

The clock in the hall said ten past seven. Davie went upstairs, washed and changed his shirt. Then he selected a bright blue tie, surveyed himself in the glass, fiddled with his hair, decided that it was almost time to give up being vain, but not quite yet, and went downstairs to dinner. He was not going to give any thought to his problems until he was fed. He gave himself over to the humours of the bill of fare. "Sherry trifle" was an old joke—sherry my foot—but "nature potatoes" was a charming piece of bastard French peculiar to the Ottery. Admirable, too, was the frank way they dealt with all those geographical poultry; "local farm Surrey fowl," the card said. It was local, all right—it came from the farm at Queen's Dodderidge. But London tradition says that fowls come from Surrey, as turkeys come from Norfolk, and ducks from Aylesbury. The Ottery preserved both truth and metropolitan tradition: their fowls were both local and Surrey.

It was endearing, and Davie did not hesitate. He ordered local Surrey fowl and found it excellent.

After dinner for a little time he studied his notes. They made nothing new to him. Tomorrow night things might wear a different look, but now . . . He looked round the lounge. Those of the widows who were awake were all deep in their novels. And yes, thought Davie, slipping the blue notebook back into his pocket, a little recreation, some refreshment to the mind, a relaxaiton to the spirit, that is precisely my need. He had it waiting in his other pocket, and it was titled *Parsnip Wine* by Sally Antrobus. The cover showed a gloved hand pouring something into a decanter. Just my glass of cordial, thought Davie.

It was midnight before he got into bed.

SEVEN

I

Sometimes, when his head was full of problems, Davie sat long over breakfast. Today there were plenty of things that might have occupied his thoughts, but only one of them held his attention. His assignation with Giles. There was nothing he could do in preparation, but he couldn't think about anything else. And midnight was a long way off. He was fidgety.

Sitting in the sun lounge, he picked up somebody's discarded paper. God, how boring it all was! The violence of criminals one could understand. But the violence of intellectuals, who were only violent because it was the fashionable thing to be, had become insufferably tedious. He turned a page, and was confronted by a strapping young woman (Jane Murcher by name and the mother of three), who had courageously sat on a fence for fifty-six hours. Was this a world record? asked our special correspondent. "No," said Davie, out loud. Suddenly he was in the happiest humour. Casting the paper aside, he heaved himself out of his chair and walked out of the room, laughing. It was only half past nine. He had decided to go for a walk.

"You see what I mean," said Mrs. Watchett, bend-

ing forward over her novel in the direction of Bea
Wimbush. "Yes, I do," said Miss Wimbush, but
rather vaguely, for she was reading a novel and knitting a jumper at the same time, and was anxious not
to lose her place in either development. "But I think
he's all right."

"Hm," said Mrs. Watchett. "I'm sure I hope so."
She was a little disappointed in Bea Wimbush.

There were not many people in the street. It was
early for shopping. Davie sauntered along as far as
the post office, and then, as he was pointing in the
right direction, he thought he would go on up West
Hill and so on to the golf links. There was a public
footpath across the links, which the golfers always
hoped would get forgotten. It would give him great
pleasure to assert his rights. And he might come
home by the cliff path.

Briskly he walked along between the generous gardens, for the old houses all had good gardens; it was
only the modern ones that had crept towards the
road, anxiously repudiating horticultural responsi-
bilities. And it was only the modern ones, because
they were near the road, which were blinded by
looped and beribboned nylon curtains, and exhibited
all those lamentable *objets* on the window sills, as
though their owners were intent on advertising their
happy understanding of what goes to make a tasteful
domestic scene. Alas for the gardens that had been
built on. A cheer for those that remained—but anyone could see that they would not remain long. Who
could keep them going?

Davie's heart was full of garden memories as he
reached the top of the hill. Indeed, it was because
he was looking towards the left at a new building in

an old garden that he did not see Ernest Stubbings standing inside the garden gate of Gonville Lodge, surveying the road with a proprietary air on this morning of July.

"Good day, sir," said Mr. Stubbings as Davie drew level.

"Good day."

"Do I have the pleasure of addressing Dr. Davie?"

"Yes. I am Dr. Davie." So Stubbings had been making enquiries.

"I," said Mr. Stubbings with evident pleasure, "am Mr. Stubbings. I have noticed you in company with young Gifford."

"Yes, Giles Gifford and I are acquainted."

"No doubt he has told you that I am chairman of our council. I had been hoping to have an opportunity of a word with your good self. And how," said Mr. Stubbings with a patronizing smile, "how do you like our little town?"

"I like it very much," said Davie. "I was born here. In the days when I knew it best we called it the village."

Mr. Stubbings laughed. "Village! Well, really you do amuse me, Dr. Davie. We have progressed a little since then, sir. Our population has much increased in recent years. We are getting rid of the older houses and building flatlets in some of the larger gardens. If only we can widen the main street by covering in the brook we shall be able to give the coaches a better chance. There is some opposition to this plan from some of the older residents, but I think my advice will prevail. If it wasn't for our stone beach we could make as fine a place of it as Torquay, but to remove the beach would be too great an undertaking.

Still, we mustn't complain, sir. Great progress is being made, under my leadership and with the help of my good friend Mr. Blizzard. Are you interested in gardens, Dr. Davie? If you are," said Mr. Stubbings, opening the garden gate, "then pray come in. You'll find it rather different from what it used to be like in your time."

"I've no doubt of that," said Davie.

For a blind moment all he could see was a picture of the apple orchard in spring, and the tumbledown cob cottage which had once stood on this site. Then, "Thank you," he said, "I would like to see it very much," and so he entered the garden, feeling less amiable towards Mr. Stubbings than he had ever felt towards anyone in his life.

As they walked up the path between stiff rows of standard roses, Davie looked at the ugly house. The door was held open by an up-ended drainpipe. It was doing service as an umbrella stand and had been disguised with painted flowers of remarkable vulgarity and improbable proportions. Beyond the drainpipe stretched an avenue of cold, shiny linoleum. Little rugs, for slipping on, lay before doorways to the right and left.

They did not go in. Mr. Stubbings turned to the right, led him round the side of the house, and brought him to the terrace which Davie had already studied through binoculars from the shelter of the elder tree.

"This is my great improvement," said Mr. Stubbings. "There used to be an old orchard here. It took me three years to get it tidy and well laid out." He pointed to the long beds that stretched down the open slope. "And at the bottom I have made a Japanese water garden. You must see it, Dr. Davie. It is the only water garden in Tidwell St. Peter's, and it cost me a pretty penny and a lot of trouble, I can tell you. More than once hooligans have tried to spoil it. On one occasion I lost one of my best storks, and a windmill."

"How very distressing," said Davie, feeling that some comment was needed after long silence. "Do you get much of this contemporary destructiveness in Tidwell St. Peter's?"

"Not much, no—but too much. Some people have lost plants. Some hedges have been damaged. One night last March somebody stole some daffodils from my front garden and, while he was about it, even helped himself to the stone which was used as my doorstop. What for? Mrs. Stubbings went down one morning to open up as usual, and the stone wasn't there. What was the sense of that? Of course it's only done for devilment."

"Was there anything particularly attractive or unusual about your stone?" asked Davie, suddenly interested.

"Mrs. Stubbings liked it. She said it had a nice pattern, but it was just an ordinary stone from the beach. Mind you, it's not Tidwell St. Peter's lads. They're well behaved. It's boys who come over from Axborough who do the damage."

"Perhaps," said Davie, "the Tidwell St. Peter's boys go over to Axborough for their entertainment."

Mr. Stubbings ignored this interruption.

"Whoever they are, if I catch them I shall not hesitate to prosecute. They've heard of me and they know that Ernest Stubbings means what he says."

Davie wondered a little if Ernest Stubbings also

said what he meant. Had he brought him here merely to serve as an audience, or did he want anything?

They were standing by the brook now, and "There!" said Mr. Stubbings. "What do you think of that? Eh? Old Challice made it—under my direction, of course. You never saw anything like that before, I'll be bound."

"Indeed I never did," said Davie.

"The true Japanese style. Pretty, isn't it?"

Davie looked beyond the pagodas and storks towards the Merrick wilderness, and without falsehood agreed that it was.

"I think so, too, sir," said Mr. Stubbings, leading the way back up the slope. "Better than the old brook, though there are some who haven't thought so. Some people will oppose anything new, Dr. Davie. That has been my difficulty all along—getting the people to look ahead, march with the times."

Back on the little terrace, Mr. Stubbings motioned Davie to a chair.

"Sit down, Dr. Davie, sit down and make yourself at home, and I'll ask Mrs. Stubbings to make us a cup of coffee."

"Thank you very much, but I never—"

"Nonsense, nonsense, I insist," said Mr. Stubbings. "Jessie!"

With an alacrity which plainly suggested that she had been standing behind the half-open back door, observing the visitor through the crack by the hinge, a woman appeared on the doorstep, a spare little woman who made not the slightest attempt to match the grand manner of her consort.

"Allow me to present you to Mrs. Stubbings," said Ernest.

"How do you do?" said Davie with an old-fashioned bow.

"Very well thank you and how are you?" said Mrs. Stubbings, as though the words were a response in the litany.

Davie had no intention of telling her. He said instead, "Your husband has very kindly been showing me the garden."

"Oh—the *garden*," said Mrs. Stubbings enigmatically, and suddenly retired into the house. Nothing had been said about coffee, but either she had overheard Mr. Stubbings's invitation, or had comprehended his desires by divination, for a few minutes later she emerged again and put two cups on the garden table.

"This is very kind," said Davie.

"Mr. Stubbings always has a cup about now. Did he show you the water garden?"

"Indeed yes."

"As long as you don't try to walk over the bridges, and keep a sharp lookout for those storks, it's quite safe," said Mrs. Stubbings, and disappeared into the house as suddenly as before. Not the slightest interpretation of her words was betrayed on her expressionless face, but after the door was shut Davie thought he could hear Mrs. Stubbings having a quiet laugh in the kitchen. He felt then that he could learn to like Mrs. Stubbings.

"You get a good view of the quarry from here," said Davie.

"Yes, and a good thing I do," said Mr. Stubbings. "It belongs to Mrs. Merrick, but it is leased to the council and we have a shed in it containing council property. On more than one occasion the windows have been broken by boys throwing stones. From here I can keep a watch on the place when at home. And from time to time I look in to see if there are any signs of trespassers."

"Have you ever caught anyone?"

"No. But I shall, Dr. Davie. I shall. The price of liberty is eternal vigilance."

"I believe," said Davie, "that there was a tragedy down there a few months ago."

Mr. Stubbings looked at him warily. "There was, sir. Mr. Merrick fell over the edge and was killed. I can't say that I was satisfied with the coroner's verdict of accidental death."

"No?"

"In my opinion, sir, it was suicide, and I will tell you why I think so, sir. Almost immediately before this accident occurred Mr. Merrick had called at my house in a great rage and was extremely rude to me about my water garden. He was hardly in his right mind, in my opinion. He left me speechless, absolutely speechless. It was only after he had gone raging out of my front gate that I could think of some of the things that I would have liked to have said in reply, and I started after him and went part way down the hill, but he was already out of sight, and so I came home again. I was glad that I did. As chairman of the council I would have been demeaning myself to argue with him."

"I thought you told the coroner that you did *not* follow him," said Davie.

Mr. Stubbings, who had been about to drink his coffee, paused with the cup halfway to his mouth, stared at Davie, and set the cup down.

"You have read the account of the inquest?"

"Yes."

"I was not *asked* if I followed Mr. Merrick, and I did *not* follow Mr. Merrick. I only *started* to follow Mr. Merrick. I did not consider, and I do not consider—"

"How far did you get?"

"About as far as Mr. Parsley's gate. Then I turned back."

"I see. That was lucky for you."

"How, 'lucky'?"

"If you had followed him, it might have been awkward after your quarrel."

"I hardly think so," said Mr. Stubbings. "People know me in Tidwell St. Peter's, sir."

"Yes, I suppose they do," said Davie, setting down his cup. He had meant to be moving, but just then there was a diversion. Over to the left, above the party hedge, a whirling spray of water rose in the air, and sparkled in the sun. "I see your neighbour's a gardener, too," he remarked.

"Mr. Parsley?" said Stubbings. "I believe so, in rather an old-fashioned way. He doesn't go in for landscape gardening or anything like that. Just lawns and flowers. He is chairman of the local Horticultural Society, so he ought to know something about it."

"That flourishes?"

"I think so. They have four shows a year, organized by Miss Gonzago."

"You don't sound very interested."

"To tell you the truth," said Mr. Stubbings, as though that were a rare privilege for him to extend to anybody, "it's a rather amateurish affair. And I don't much like the way it's run. This is a small place, Dr. Davie. We can't afford to have scandals."

"Scandals? Do you mean cornering the prizes?"

"No, Dr. Davie, not that. Improprieties. Mr. Parsley and Miss Gonzago—"

"Oh go on!" said Davie, laughing softly. "You don't mean—"

"But I do, sir, certainly I do. I will give you an example which has especially remained in my mind, partly because of the date. We were talking just now of the night that Mr. Merrick was killed. Of course I knew nothing of that till the next day." (Exactly what Arthur Parsley had said, thought Davie in parenthesis.) "But after the unpleasantness with Mr. Merrick I had felt quite unable to sleep. So I had sat up late, doing my council work. Then, before going to bed, at about midnight I came out here on the terrace for a breath of air. I had just been walking quietly across the grass towards the hedge, when I was suddenly attracted by a sound on the other side. Thinking that it might have been one of these hooligans, I tiptoed up to the hedge and looked through at a point near to Mr. Parsley's gate—and what do you think I saw?"

"I expect you mean *whom* do I think you saw."

"There in the moonlight," said Mr. Stubbings in a low dramatic voice, "was Miss Gonzago. *Past twelve o'clock,* Dr. Davie. Just leaving Mr. Parsley's gate and going back down the hill. I can tell you, Dr. Davie, I did not think it at all nice, and nor did Mrs. Stubbings. We can't afford that sort of behaviour in a small place like this, sir. I am not one to talk, Dr. Davie, and you may be sure I have kept this entirely to myself. Entirely. But you will understand that I have no wish to associate myself with the Tidwell St. Peter's Horticultural Society."

"Indeed I do see that," said Davie, adding, as he looked at his watch, "Goodness! It's nearly eleven. I must be off." Mr. Stubbings accompanied him to the gate. "Please thank Mrs. Stubbings for my coffee," said Davie. "And thank *you* for showing me the garden. It was interesting."

"I knew you would enjoy it," said Mr. Stubbings. But that was not quite what Davie had said.

II

It was too late now to take the path across the golf links. After a moment's hesitation he turned back towards the village. Mr. Stubbings's observations had not been wholly without interest. He thought he might sit an hour in the Ottery garden and consider them.

It was ten past eleven when he reached the post office. The high shopping hour had begun. If you knew people in Tidwell St. Peter's it was impossible to make your way without a constant repetition of "Morning" and "Another lovely day" and all those other passwords which enable people to pass. The street was abuzz with amiable comments on the weather.

Davie knew nobody now, except a few shopkeepers, and, in a manner, Basil Jason and Mrs. Merrick. He did not expect to have to say anything to anyone, but there, as luck would have it, right in his path, was Mrs. Merrick. She was talking to somebody on the pavement outside Blizzard and Harbottle. He did not want to give the appearance of avoiding her, and so he kept on his way, but he did not want to meet her, and so he assumed an interest in the opposite side of the road. It was not necessary. Just before he drew level Mrs. Merrick broke away from her friend and disappeared into Turpin's. Not, he presumed, for coffee and cakes—a woman of Mrs. Merrick's graceful figure would know better—but for something to take home for a more suitable time of day.

So far as Davie was concerned, Turpin's was a new shop. Davie's mother had always gone to Wonnacott's further down the street, and, such is conservatism, such is tradition, the older residents still went to Wonnacott's, even though Turpin's did purvey a creamier kind of cake and a shinier sort of bun. The older residents were not to be seduced. There was nothing (they used to say) like Mrs. Wonnacott's sponges.

Five minutes later, as he settled down in a chair in the Ottery garden, he was still smiling to himself over "the older residents" and their notorious prejudices. Sixty years ago, when Bissicker had moved in (only from West Tidwell) and had opened an ironmonger's shop in High Street, Davie's mother had not only forbidden the family to go near the place, but, in a demonstration of sympathy and unwavering loyalty, had immediately purchased a number of unnecessary articles from Barnes, the old ironmonger. Those were the days, thought Davie. The friendly days.

Then he put his hand in his pocket and drew out the blue notebook.

STUBBINGS (he wrote): I think this offensive little man is so totally taken up with his own importance that he thinks of nothing else. His explanation why he takes such an interest in the quarry sounds convincing to me. Giles said he was the aboriginal prodnose; I think he is perhaps also the prototype red herring. He could have been involved in Merrick's death—he was in the right place and had the wrong motives—but, unless I find better evidence, I just don't think that he was involved.

The patronizing attitude towards Arthur Parsley as a gardener is obviously jealousy and injured pride. Mr. S. thinks that *he* ought to be chairman of the Horticultural Society.

Far more interesting than Stubbings himself are two things that he said. First, that he had lost his doorstop. As he suggests, it was probably pinched by one of the boys. And it certainly wasn't the stone I found: that came from a wall. But beach stones seem to be forcing themselves on my attention. It will be confusing to find too many of them.

His other observation is much more to the point. At something near midnight on the night of Merrick's death, Stubbings alleges that he saw Miss Gonzago leaving Rose Cottage. He draws moral conclusions; but if moral conclusions are all that can be found I am not remotely interested. What *is* surely interesting is this: Miss Gonzago lived in the separate wing at Pinewood; she must have known about Merrick's death. The obvious assumption is that she came down in the night watches to inform Arthur Parsley. Like Mrs. Merrick, she could have telephoned. But she did not. This introduces a new character on the scene. It also casts a new light on Arthur Parsley. He told me that he knew nothing about Merrick's death until Rachel Merrick called on him in the morning. It now looks as though he may have known all about it many hours before. If he did know, why did he need to lie? And what is Miss Gonzago's interest in the matter? The problem has suddenly become wider.

Davie read over what he had written, drew one of his final lines across the page, and put the notebook in his pocket. It wanted forty minutes to luncheon. Time for a short walk. Down the street, along the parade to the first shelter, and back by the cliff path. And yes, said Dr. Davie to his heart, let's do that—provided we can get out of this damned low chair.

III

Miss Gonzago, at that hour, was getting ready for her picnic, bobbing to and fro, as occasion demanded, between the shop and the little kitchen behind it.

She had had a busy morning. There had been customers, one of whom had bought the bead footstool. There had been callers, one of whom had been Mr. Parsley. He had wanted a word about the autumn chrysanthemum show.

"The arrangements," said Miss Gonzago, "will be just the same as usual. They always work very well."

"Perfectly."

"And they are all in hand."

"I knew they would be. You're as steady as a clock. But I always feel I ought to ask. It makes me believe that the chairman is really doing something."

"You do a great deal, Mr. Parsley," said Miss Gonzago. "I don't know where we would be without you."

There was a barometer hanging on the wall. Mr. Parsley consulted it.

"Does this work?"

"Indeed it does."

"Then the weather stays fair."

"Yes. And I'm going to take my tea on the beach, where I hope that my nephew and his wife will be joining me."

Miss Gonzago paused and pointed at someone passing down the street. "Can you tell me who that is?" she asked. "There. The gentleman."

"Yes, I can. He's a Dr. Davie. He used to live here as a boy and he's staying at the Ottery. Giles Gifford brought him to see me. That's how I know."

"I wondered. He was looking in at the window yesterday. And later, when I went up to the end of the garden, I saw him sitting on a cliff bench. He was talking to old Challice."

"He's a great talker. I'm surprised he hasn't called on you. He's interested in antiques. I must be off. Have a nice picnic."

Miss Gonzago accompanied him to the door.

"Goodbye, Mr. Parsley," she said with one of her gentle spiritual smiles, but, even as she spoke, she was thinking that she ought to get the little saucepan on, or she would be late skinning the tomatoes.

As Arthur Parsley walked up the street towards

West Hill it was Davie who occupied his thoughts. So he had been talking to Challice. He'd been to see Pinewood—but surely not because he really wanted to rent it. He had called twice at Rose Cottage. Earlier that morning he had caught a glimpse of him inspecting the Stubbings water garden. He was making a great point of talking to everyone. But not apparently to Miss Gonzago, who might have been able to tell him about that snowstorm.

There could only be one reason for talking to Challice, thought Arthur Parsley, as he drew level with the open door of the Angel . . . But there his thoughts were diverted. It was the right time of day for a drink. Three steps and he was inside. In the blare of vacuous conversation which greeted him Arthur Parsley forgot, temporarily, about Dr. Davie.

As soon as Arthur Parsley had gone, Miss Gonzago slipped into the little kitchen and put the kettle on. She also put on two small saucepans of water. She put three eggs into one of these. The other was for blanching the tomatoes. Most people can't be bothered to skin a tomato. You only have to dip it into boiling water for a few seconds and the skin comes off like a glove. Miss Gonzago liked things done well, and so she dipped four tomatoes in the water, skinned them, and sliced them. Then she looked around for the brown loaf and realized that she had forgotten to bring it. Normally Miss Gonzago bought her bread at Turpin's, but Wonnacott's was only two minutes up the road, so there was no difficulty. But it was Thursday and, except for the café, the shop would be shut at one o'clock. It behoved Miss Gonzago to step up the road quickly: so she locked the door, and bother the customers, thought Miss Gonzago with gay bravado, though her face wore its customary expression of humble resignation, bother the customers, and anyhow I don't suppose there will be any.

"A brown loaf, please," said Miss Gonzago, and, because she felt a little awkward about Turpin's, she added, "and one of your lovely sponges. Nobody makes a sponge like you, Mrs. Wonnacott."

"I mind when old Mrs. Wonnacott taught me how to make that sponge," said Mrs. Wonnacott. "That was fifty years ago, and I've been making them ever since."

"And we're all so grateful," said Miss Gonzago, and then, suddenly remembering the kettle, she hurried back to the shop. There wasn't much water left in it, so she filled the kettle again, and while it boiled she sat down to a mild lunch of cream cheese and biscuits with a glass of sherry. Then she made the tea in two large thermos flasks (because Dick and Christine were expected) and put the tomato sandwiches and the boiled eggs and the sponge cake into cellophane bags, and packed them all into a big tea basket. Then, at two o'clock precisely, she walked up the garden, and out, by the back gate, on to the cliff path.

As she passed the Ottery garden she noticed the elderly gentleman, Dr. Davie, sitting in the garden after lunch. And Dr. Davie, who was not yet asleep, noticed Miss Gonzago. He wondered where she was going, all alone, with her big tea basket.

IV

For an hour he slept in the garden. It was quiet there. The old ladies were all lying down; the younger visitors were on the beach, or playing tennis, or somewhere far away in their cars. The waves and the gulls made background music—anyone could sleep to those sounds—but when a gull alighted in the garden and very deliberately said squark for Davie's (as it seemed) special attention, then he did wake up and look at his watch. It was three o'clock. There were still nine hours to use before his appointment with Giles, and nothing particular to do in them. There had been nothing particular to do in the morning, but the morning had been fruitful. Maybe it would be rewarding if he went out for the walk he hadn't taken earlier in the day. He got himself out of his chair, went to his room to collect the binoculars, passed the time of day with Miss Mingo at reception, and walked through the garden to the cliff. At the gate he turned to the right and started up the steep path towards the beacon, the path he had taken on his first evening in Tidwell St. Peter's, the path to the Chine.

At regular intervals benches had been placed by beneficent town councils of the long past, and Davie sat down on every one of them on his way up to the long level field, which divides the first ascent from the final rising track to the beacon. From each position he surveyed the beach and the bay through his glasses. There were many people bathing. Further out a motorboat was towing a young man on water skis. In the distance small boats were sailing. Far away a larger vessel was slowly moving along the horizon.

The path was stiff going. He was glad when he got to the level field.

For him that field was forever associated with butterflies, the little pale blue ones, and the deep rose with black dots and black edges to their wings. He could remember trying to catch them in his hands when he was about three. He remembered the wild scabious too.

There were no butterflies there now, partly because the field was a football ground, but mostly because, some years ago, there had been a plant disease which had destroyed the green thing that the butterflies liked best. They had moved away. But where to? It seemed to Davie that never again anywhere had he seen those little butterflies, the pale blue and the deep rose.

So, with his thoughts full of butterflies, he crossed the field, and followed the further path, between great clumps of gorse, until he came near to the sea again, where the track marches with the cliff. And there he turned left, down the steep narrow path to that secret seat, perched on the edge of the cliff. Below him, where the Chine made a gash in the sandstone like a V, the land sloped away covered in gorse and blackthorn. From here, framed in that V, he could see a segment of the bay and part of the beach below the cliff. There was, he noticed, one person sitting on the beach close to the sea, occasionally shying pebbles into the water: a woman. She must have had a long tramp on the stones to get there—or a hard scramble down the Chine.

Davie raised his binoculars and looked out to sea. In the part he was able to scan there was nothing at all; and then, a moment later, something exhilarating and swift flashed over the water. It was the motorboat drawing the young man on skis. Then he disappeared as suddenly, and a few seconds later passed again, further out, as the motorboat turned in a great circle. Another few seconds and he was gone again. Davie felt envious. That was something Robert and he had never done, and Robert would have been so good at it.

Presently he heard the chugging of the motorboat again. But she was moving more soberly now, and when she appeared a few seconds later he saw that she was heading for the beach. A young woman was at the controls, and the nearly naked young man was standing up, waving a friendly hand at the woman on the beach. The woman stood up and waved back.

Slowly the boat nosed in to shore. Then the young man jumped out with a painter and a stake, which he drove firmly into the pebbles, and then, since the boat could not come in absolutely to the water's edge, for the waves foamed far up the sloping beach, he returned to the boat and carried the young lady through the shallows while the young lady carried in her arms what was obviously a tea basket. Davie looked at the trio through the glasses and suddenly realized that the welcoming lady on the beach was Miss Gonzago. She had not been off on a lonely picnic. She had been expecting these young ones, the young ones had been expecting her, and they, too, had brought offerings. Miss Gonzago kissed both of them, and they kissed her. There was a lot of gay laughter on the pebbles as the three gathered round to take their tea from the two baskets.

Davie sat on, scanning the bay through the glasses, but nothing else passed by, except a ship far out to sea. Then, as he was beginning to think of turning home—it was indeed teatime—he heard steps on the little path. Someone else was coming down to the secret seat. You could not pass on that path. So he waited. And presently round the edge of the blackthorn came Arthur Parsley.

"Good gracious!" said Mr. Parsley.

"What-ho!" said Davie.

"You are a wizard, Dr. Davie. You know everything about Tidwell St. Peter's, even its solitary places."

"Lord love you," said Davie, "there's nothing remarkable in that. I've known this particular solitary place since I was so high."

Arthur Parsley sat down beside him. He said, "I often come here and hardly anyone else does—except the loving young, and that's usually by moonlight. How much longer are you staying?"

"Not more than a day or so. It's been a great pleasure to come down. But I have other calls."

"You've finished your researches?"

"Researches?" It was an unexpected word.

"At Cadleigh, I mean."

"Oh *that*. Yes, I'm pretty satisfied there."

"And now Lady Cassillis has gone away," said Parsley.

"How news gets around," said Davie quietly. He had no notion that Irene had gone away.

"I assumed it," said Parsley. "About noon yesterday I was coming back from Axborough and I passed them on the road—Donald driving. There was a lot baggage. Hence my inside information."

"It's an excellent thing that she should go," said Davie. "She's been living at great strain."

"I don't know her well," said Parsley. "But I think she's a good thing."

"Certainly," said Davie. "An admirable person."

Down on the beach the young people were preparing to return to the motorboat. They knelt heads together repacking the baskets. Miss Gonzago collected used bags and paper napkins and put them in one big bag. Then she added a stone and threw the whole thing into the sea. Davie could see that Parsley was aware of the activities going on below them, but he did not refer to them, so Davie let it pass. Miss Gonzago's picnic was not a particularly fruitful subject for conversation. "Time I got back," he said, rising. "Goodbye."

"Goodbye. Careful of that path. It's steep, slippery, narrow, thorny, stony—"

"I know, but after that it's downhill all the way. I'll be all right."

On the way home Dr. Davie pondered a good deal about Mr. Parsley. And Mr. Parsley, sitting privately on the cliff's edge, returned to his morning speculations, and pondered a good deal about Dr. R. V. Davie. And neither of them reached any satisfactory conclusion.

V

Davie finished his tea and looked at his watch. Never had he enquired the time so often as he had that day. It was nearly five. There were still seven hours to fill. One of them he spent finishing *Parsnip Wine*. It was not often that he was bamboozled by a crime story writer, but he was bound to admit that Sally Antrobus had been extremely sly. She had dropped her vital clue in the first chapter and had never gone back to it. With the result, dammit, that he had failed to recognize that Sir George and Professor Crabbit were one person. Really (with *Edwin Drood* in mind) he ought to have spotted that wig. It was not often that Davie was had like that. He attributed his lapse to the fact that he had been interrupted by graver concerns. But he raised his hat to Miss Antrobus. She had played her hand well.

From six to six-thirty he indulged in a minor kind of doze. But at six-thirty his course was plainly indicated. It was reasonable at that hour to seek a glass of the usual.

Basil Jason was in the bar, talking to a young lady wearing a minimal miniskirt and perched on a stool to enhance the effect. Davie nodded to Jason, and Jason nodded to him. He did not offer him a share in the young lady's conversation, which chiefly consisted, as far as Davie could hear, in peals of laughter and cries of "Really, Basil!" and "You are awful" and other such repartees from a young lady's six o'clock repertoire. Basil Jason appeared to be delighted with her.

"But Basil, you are a bore," said Pansy Packenham (for she was none other), "you *must* come to Mummy's cocktail party. She'll *never* forgive you if you don't."

"But I can't, sweetheart," said Basil. "I've got a job to do."

"Fiddle!"

"I have—and it takes me away tomorrow for two or three days. I can't help it."

"Well, I think you're a pig," said Pansy Packenham.

"I think pigs are nice," said Basil.

But that was as much as Davie heard of this conversation. By then more people had come into the bar, and a curtain of sound arose between him and Pansy Packenham. At times, through the haze, he would see her throw her head back in a paroxysm of laughter, or droop forward so that her hair fell over her face, but he was excluded from the enjoyment of what was evidently an excessively witty interchange of opinion. It was, he thought, a little selfish of Basil Jason.

He knew nobody else in the bar, so he sat down quietly in a corner, and, thinking about many things, lost himself for a while, not heeding at all the buzz of talk around him. It was a familiar voice which recalled him to the present.

"So I said to him straight out, 'Village! You really do amuse me. We have progressed a little since then, sir.'" It was Mr. Stubbings relating his day's experiences for the edification of Mr. Smallpiece and anyone else within earshot.

"But he was a good sort of chap, so I offered to show him round. He was much impressed, I can tell you. He didn't expect anything like a Japanese garden down here."

Davie was near the door, and he had finished his drink. Three steps and he was back in the hotel. As he closed the door he heard Mr. Smallpiece saying, "You had him there, Mr. Stubbings."

VI

At about the time when Davie entered the bar at the Ottery, Irene was trying to write a letter in the sitting room of a private suite in that very delectable and deliberately old-fashioned London hotel, the Dorset. Up to 1939 the Dorset had made a charming pretence of expecting carriage folk by scrupulously maintaining a sanded area outside the front portal for the cleaner accommodation of the horses which had not been seen there or anywhere else in London since about 1920. The sand has gone now, but the county atmosphere is still carefully preserved within. The Dorset is a collector's piece, and intends to remain so. Foreign visitors, with some justification, regard it as a part of Old England. We shall not look upon its like again.

Of course the Dorset does not overdo the old-world atmosphere. The architecture and the courtesies are old-fashioned, but the comforts are new. The lacquered cabinet, for instance, in Irene's sitting room, has never seen the eighteenth century, and when its doors are opened, instead of a series of exciting drawers and pigeonholes, it displays glasses and bottles and all the apparatus for mixing shameful drinks. You get the best of both worlds at the Dorset, and the upholstery belongs to this one.

At the writing table in the window Irene tore a letter up and dropped the pieces in the wastepaper basket. It was her seventh attempt. Then she took another piece of paper and began again.

> My dear R.V.
>
> I feel absolutely terrible about this. What will you think of me—leaving Cadleigh without a word. I had made my mind up yesterday, when I saw you. But I couldn't tell you because if I had I would also have had

And there it was again. She could not get past that point.

And then Donald came in. He was straight out of the bath, his hair disordered, wearing a blue and white dressing gown. He went to the lacquered cabinet, exposed its undignified interior, and mixed two glasses of whisky and water. He took one to Irene at the writing table.

"How are you getting on?" he asked.

"I'm not," said Irene. "The facts are simple, but I can't put them simply. I wish you'd write it."

"Wouldn't he dislike that?"

"I don't think so. He's understanding."

"Perhaps you could add something at the end."

"Yes—but it must go tonight."

"All right. I'll have a shot at it."

So Irene took her drink to the sofa, and Donald sat down at the writing table. Fifteen minutes later he took a piece of paper to Irene and said, "Will this do? It's the best I can manage."

Irene read the letter.

"Yes," she said. "That will do. I knew you'd write it better than I could. I'll just add a line at the end —and please get dressed and get it posted. There isn't much time, and it must go tonight."

VII

Eight-thirty P.M. There were still three-and-a-half hours to fill. First he started a new novel. It was the title which had hooked him: *The Man in the Attic.* But alas, the man in the attic was not, as he had reasonably supposed, a spy. He ought to have read the blurb, which explained that this brilliant book likened mankind to the rooms of a house. So far as Davie could see, nearly all of them lived on the bedroom floor. He was amazed. Here in his hand lay the evidence for the genuine purity of the anti-censorship campaign. Censored this book would have been passed from hand to hand with gasping astonishment. Free, it went from hand to wastepaper basket. The boredom was total. The author had missed the bus by about ten years. Davie gave up, exhausted. Gave up and got up, and went into the television room.

"When they told me about Bob I felt—you know."

A brave little woman was being interviewed about her husband's accident. But no one was ever to learn how she did feel about it because in the end she always assumed that—you know—they knew already.

"Well—I'm trying to be—you know," said the brave little woman. And dear God! Davie was thinking, this appalling fungus which defiles the English language, this loathsome conversational ineptitude, this drivelling disruption of human communication, this —you know. But happily there is a limit to what cannot be known in an interview, and suddenly the brave little woman disappeared with a winsome smile and in her place there sailed into the box most gloriously a Western, a genuine Western, sheriff and all. "Praise the Lord!" said Davie aloud, and watched the whole thing from start to finish with eager anxiety for the cause of justice.

"An excellent story," said an elderly lady as she left the room.

"Yes, indeed," said Davie, for the end of a film breaks down all barriers and he had no compunction in addressing her without an introduction. "My heart was in my mouth. But there was one curious thing about it. Did you observe what bad shots all those villains were? There they were blazing away at one man dodging among the rocks—they could put a bullet through his hat, they could hit some unimportant dago who was dodging about with him, but they could never hit our favourite. I don't think they were much good as villains, do you?"

"Oh yes, they were," said the old lady. "They were very bad men indeed. But they met their match. Life is very different in the western states of America, you know."

"Ah yes," said Davie. "I dare say it is."

At half past ten he went up to his room, took the stone from his corner drawer—the stone with the girdle of mortar around it—and laid it carefully in

Giles's basket. Then he went downstairs, basket in hand, collected his raincoat, and sat down in the outer lounge. By now the place was empty, but he was able to order a pot of coffee. Drinking that and reading the remains of several newspapers occupied him till twenty to twelve. Then, making sure that the hall porter was nowhere near, he unlocked the garden door and let himself out. He did not feel that he was endangering the lives and property of his fellow guests. No one would know that the door was open. Then he crossed the garden and let himself out on to the cliff path.

There were lights in the hotel further up the cliff. But otherwise Tidwell St. Peter's was abed. For a minute he stood there, listening to the waves. Then he turned to the left and strolled slowly down towards the parade.

At five minutes to twelve, at the old wall, the wall of Ambrose Faddle's celebrated picture, he turned left and walked quietly up the street. There was nobody and no thing in sight. The West Tidwell Road was the first on the right. As he turned into it the car went slowly past him and stopped by the curb.

A hand opened the door.

In Fore Street the clock on the Methodist church struck twelve.

"Well met," said Davie.

"You said the West Tidwell Road," said Giles in an unnecessary whisper.

"Yes. I'll tell you what I want as we drive."

"Right," said Giles. "Here we go."

Twenty seconds later they had left the village behind them.

"Go the way we went that first evening—Clumber

Rise, then down the hill, and hairpin back along the road that passes the quarry. But we'll have to park some distance before we get to it."

"Before or after Basil Jason's house?"

"Before. I don't want anyone to notice the car. We'll have to walk the rest of it."

"Where to?"

"Rose Cottage. It would have been quicker up West Hill—but there are too many houses that way."

"And when we get there? We're not—"

"We're not calling on Arthur Parsley. No. We're going to see whether this stone fits exactly into the cavity on top of his gatepost."

"Oho!" said Giles. "Are we?"

Clearly there was nothing more to say about that and for two minutes they drove in silence. Then, "What sort of hours does Arthur Parsley keep?"

"I'm not sure. He was one of the people at this dinner party. He'd have been home by eleven."

"It will be half past twelve by the time we get there."

After that neither of them spoke again until Giles drew into the side of the road by a convenient field gate. "I can't go any further," he said. "This is the last gap where I can get the car off the road. And I'll have to leave the lights on."

"Before we get out let's understand exactly what we've got to do. There ought not to be any trouble. The experiment shouldn't take more than a minute. We could be back here in fifteen minutes. We've got to be absolutely quiet. I may have to speak to you at the gate. But don't you speak unless I need an answer."

"Right."

"When we get there I'll give you the basket to hold. First I'll take out the loose stone from the top of the pillar and hand it to you. Then I'll take the other stone from our basket and fit it in. When it's in I'll have to put on the torch to see if it fits. If it does fit I take it out and give it to you again and you give me back the other stone. I put it back and we return."

"And if it doesn't fit?"

"I try again. I might have got it the wrong way round."

"And if it still doesn't fit?"

"Then the whole thing's a washout. Come on. How does this blasted door open?"

Giles leant across him and opened it.

"Have you room to get out?"

"Just."

Giles closed and locked the doors gently. Then they stood together in the lane, and listened. Freezing its quarry with that dreadful cry, an owl was hunting in Cadleigh woods. A light wind ruffled the trees.

They set off down the lane, not speaking, walking carefully, and again the owl cried from a nearer field. Most creatures stalk their victims silently, thought Davie. But the owl's like Genghis Khan, or Hitler, or Stalin: he advertises what he's going to do, and the victim hears, and waits for him to do it.

A minute's walk brought them to the turning on the left, the leafy lane which leads to Pinewood. Almost opposite, on the other side of the road, Basil Jason's house stood dark against the sky. Then the trees came closer to them, the pine trees in Merrick's woods, and on the other side the great beeches and oaks of Cadleigh. It was dark walking between the trees, for there was no moon, only the stars.

It was lighter when they came to the open quarry. And then the road dipped down to the familiar brook and up towards the Exeter road.

Halfway up the hill was a stationary light. "What's that?" asked Davie, suddenly stopping.

"A car."

It was parked not exactly outside Rose Cottage, but only a little further up the hill. It seemed that they were possibly unlucky. It seemed that Arthur Parsley had a visitor, though the front side of the house was dark.

RTK 549H. Davie knew nothing about cars. Except for a Rolls, he could not distinguish one make from another. But he had an infallible memory for numbers. He made mnemonics out of them and useless little stories. For Davie RTK spelt Arctic and 5 plus 4 equalled 9. For two seconds he saw icebergs and nine polar bears. Then "Damn it," he whispered as they reached Rose Cottage. "Whose is it?"

"I've never seen it before," said Giles. "It looks new."

"We must risk it," said Davie. "At least the house is dark."

To Giles, as he stood there holding the basket in one hand, and then, presently, a stone in the other, the overwhelming presence was the smell of Arthur Parsley's garden. It was roses, it was honeysuckle, it was tobacco plant. And then Davie switched his torch on for a seocnd, and the gatepost stood sharply against the hedge.

"Drat it," said Davie under his breath. Then he pocketed the torch, and Giles knew that he was facing the stone the other way. When he flashed the torch again, Giles heard him say, "It *is* the stone—I can see from the line of the mortar. But it still doesn't fit. I'm going to put it in the basket a minute and fiddle inside."

After a few seconds Davie said, "Now, give it to me." Then the torch flashed again for a second, and Giles heard him say in a faraway voice, "Glory be!" Then he felt the weight of the stone as Davie replaced it in the basket, and Davie's hand as he took the other stone away from him.

Five seconds later they were walking back down the hill towards the brook, the stone—the stone with the girdle of mortar—in the basket, and in Davie's pocket some paper thing he had picked out of the socket and hadn't wanted to drop on the road: a bit of stuffing, a something which had helped the stone that didn't belong there, but had hindered the one that did.

As they started up the hill towards the quarry, a light rain began to fall. "No harm in this," said Davie softly. "If we've left marks on the gravel they can do with a wash."

VIII

If they had not known the road so well, both of them, they would have felt lost, so dark it was now between the trees.

> Like one that on a lonesome road
> Doth walk in fear and dread . . .

Whenever he was on a lonesome road, Davie always thought of those lines, and they never failed to send a shiver down his back. He was glad he was not alone now, with that dreadful owl, too—straight from *Macbeth*.

But soon they were at the top of the rise. Ahead, on the left, they could just see Jason's house, a little darker than the sky. And here on the right were the gorse bushes by the public path through the pine trees. Only another two minutes, thought Davie, and we're through.

And then, "Listen!" said Giles, suddenly. "There's a car coming."

"I don't—"

"There *is*—quick!"

Giles pulled him out of the road and pushed him down behind a gorse bush.

"He hadn't quite made the top. He can't have seen us. Listen!"

And then Davie heard it too, and presently saw the lights, searching the hills and valleys in the road, probing the hedges, discovering the crinkled bark of pine trees, and the green leaves of the oaks. For a second they pierced the gorse bushes. And then the car went slowly by, and the darkness returned like a shutter.

Giles and Davie stood up and stepped back on the road.

"Why was he going so slowly?" asked Davie.

"If he's going to West Tidwell, he'll see the car. That's certain," said Giles.

"Why was he going so slowly?" repeated Davie. "Looking for something?"

"He might have lost his way."

"Or was it journey's end?" said Davie.

He had been watching the red light, and suddenly it had disappeared. "I don't think he was going to West Tidwell. I think he was going to Basil Jason's."

"Probably *was* Basil Jason. I couldn't see the car."

"Let's go on," said Davie. "We can't stay here."

"There's a light," said Giles. "It was Jason, all right."

"Or someone calling on him."

Walking one behind the other, close to the hedge, they got as near to the gate as they could and peered through the beeches planted on the bank. That was easy. In any hedge there are always gaps near the roots, and these roots were at eye level.

Their opportunity lasted one minute. The door of the house stood open, a light shone in the porch, and Basil Jason was standing by the open boot of the car. Another man, his back towards the hedge, pulled out two suitcases and carried them into the house. Then Jason shut down the boot, followed him in, shut the front door and snapped out the light.

As they drove back to the Ottery, Davie said, "I know you're longing to hear what I've got out of tonight's doings. I don't know, Giles. Not at this time of the morning. But if I fit anything together I'll tell you."

"All right, Dr. Davie, I'll be patient."

Then, after a minute's silence, Giles said, "I wonder who that was with Jason—we only got his back view."

"Which included his ears," said Davie.

Giles turned his head, a question in his eyes. But Davie did not elaborate; he was thinking of something else. Jason had told the girl in the Ottery bar that he was going away. But he wasn't loading up; he was unloading. Well—that was sense. Even in the depths of the country it's a fool who leaves possessions in a car. How many times has one heard that radio police call? Stolen from the back of a car, diplomatic papers, doctor's case, dangerous drugs . . . No—there was nothing really in that.

But it had been interesting to recognize so soon RTK 549H. And why had it been waiting outside Rose Cottage?

EIGHT

I

Dr. Davie was an early waker. He was generally alive by six o'clock. But then he would turn over and drop into a half doze, and this was his hour of fantasies. Sometimes these would be pure entertainment worthy of a psychiatrist's solemn attention. Sometimes, between sleeping and waking, he would observe his problems from another angle, and then he would sit up in bed suddenly and say, "Of course."

This morning, as he lay there, half asleep, he was listening to the waves, advancing and retreating on the beach below the cliff, for the wind had changed and the sea sounded rough. That dragging noise of the Tidwell stones brought Robert into his thoughts (it always did): Robert lying at the water's edge, and the foam racing to cover him up, and turning back again, shifting the pebbles this way, that way, monotonously. And then, thinking of the beach sixty years back set him wondering—as it had a few days earlier—about old Stapleton, the smuggling parson, and Tidwell St. Peter's in the days of brandy kegs. You couldn't do that today—too many people. And then, no, he thought, not too many people: too many kegs. Too many big things. But it isn't always kegs, he thought. And it isn't always big. Diamonds, for instance. Diamonds aren't big. And dope isn't big. Dope is small. You could put it in your pocket, in your handbag, in . . . But he did not complete that exposition of the dope traffic, because he suddenly went to sleep for ten minutes and had a rather nice dream about an elephant.

If you can land twenty-five Pakistanis on the coast of Kent, he presently informed himself, and get away with it, you can land other things. And then he began thinking how he would set about the job himself —and then, suddenly, there he was, sitting up in bed and saying, "Of course," after which he said, "Not 'of course.' Just an idea." But it was a good enough idea to get him out of bed.

It was twenty past seven. He crossed the room, drew the curtains and looked out over the garden to the sea. The bay was full of white horses, the garden full of sunshine. Dr. Davie never got up more quickly in his life. He was out on the cliff by eight.

The sea was more noisy than rough. A ground swell was dragging at the pebbles. The glorious morning was not going to last. Black clouds were building up in the southwest. The rain was coming.

Davie sat down on a bench and considered the reason for his speedy uprising. Things that seem exciting and reasonable in a drowsy head will declare difficulties and inadequacies on closer inspection. There have been so many jokes about lines that poets have scribbled feverishly at two o'clock in the morning on the note pads waiting by their beds. "How lovely in the spring is your thing, how beautiful in the autumn . . ." Davie recalled an ancient undergraduate bawdry. His waking inspiration was less clear in his head now. An easy way to smuggle small things, yes.

But that was not proof that anyone was doing anything of the sort. It was only an entertaining fantasy.

Now that he was wide awake, his thoughts were naturally more engaged by last night's experiences. There were facts there which were not open to any dispute. The stone that he had found at the gravel pit fitted into the slot on top of Arthur Parsley's gatepost. Someone had taken it away. Someone had put another stone in its place. It had seemed enormously improbable that he would ever find where the first stone had come from; but he had done so. It had come from a place very near to the scene of the crime. The person who took it must have known Rose Cottage well—well enough to know that the stone was loose. But here now was a second problem. Where had the new stone come from? If only he could find that out . . . It might have come direct from the beach. But he did not think so. In an emergency, which the filling of that gap was evidently considered to be, a person would surely have taken something immediately to hand. Not immediately to hand at the time of the catastrophe. On the edge of the quarry there would not have been a beach stone immediately to hand. No, immediately to hand when the person was safely home and ready to think about it. That created a problem almost impossible to solve. Unless Arthur Parsley was the person who put it in position (the obvious supposition, but why hadn't he mortared it in, tidy man that he was?), the second stone might have come from anywhere in Tidwell St. Peter's.

Anywhere, and yet the queer thing was that last night when he had seen it by the light of the torch he'd had a feeling that the stone was one he had actually seen somewhere or other before. He could make no sense of that. He had come to a dead end.

For a few more minutes he watched the white horses in the bay and the gulls wheeling and calling. They were looking for breakfast. Then he looked at his watch; it was half past eight. He was ready for breakfast, too. He walked back through the flowers to the hotel.

Like most English hotels the Ottery was great on breakfast. None of your continental abstemiousness here. Even if a little breakfast is what one prefers, one ends up inevitably under the discipline of that unchanging menu with its five different forms of egg, the bacon, the fruit juices, the cereals, the toast. Davie did not hesitate. He was paying for it, and, like nearly everyone else, he ordered, and was cheerfully supplied with the lot.

This morning he took a long time over breakfast, and before he left the table he put his hand in his pocket and drew out the blue notebook. He had meant to write down some of his thinking before he forgot it, but there inside the cover he found that chunk of paper which he had retrieved from the road by Arthur Parsley's gate. It was an ordinary, and rather dirty paper bag, not one proclaiming the primacy of Pearcey's Stores, just a plain bag, and it was much mangled. He unfolded it.

It would be a good bag to blow up and bang, thought Davie—a thought which, like so many other thoughts, transported him to childhood days in Tidwell St. Peter's. Always, as a ritual, they had blown up and banged the bags which held the farthing buns which they took to the beach to eat after bathing. He would have liked very much to bang this one, but that was an impossible indulgence, partly because the thing might turn out to be evidence of something or other and must be preserved, partly because he did not wish to be responsible for the premature deaths of several elderly ladies, sitting over a last cup of coffee, and already deep in the novels from which they were never parted, not even at meal times.

Instead, therefore, of banging it, he smoothed it out on the table without thinking very much what he was doing, and it was indeed creased, not only from his folding, but also from having been screwed round the stone in the slot on the top of the pillar. When he had finished one side, he turned the bag over and smoothed the other side, and it was only then that he noticed the writing in the corner.

13th & Sео farr

Davie examined the characters. They were not difficult to decipher. The 13th was presumably a date. What did the rest mean? He opened the bag and peered into the corners. He could not see anything. Then he reversed it on the table and gently agitated the bag. Then he turned it up again and examined the white cloth. He wished, for an embarrassed moment, that he had that magnifying glass which is so important a part of a sleuth's traditional baggage. But even without its aid he could distinguish what had dropped from a far corner of the bag. It was a small, dry, elderly crumb. There had been buns, or

cakes, or scones in that bag—and yes, scones it was—
"sco," scones, six scones. And the squiggle beginning
with a G—or was it an S, or an F?—doubtless indicated where they were going. It was a flat interpretation. For a moment it had looked like something
exciting, a message of some kind. But a message would
have been written on a small piece of paper, not
an undisciplined bag, and it would have been removed by the recipient. Alas, someone had bought
and paid for six scones on the 13th, and that was
all the bag had to report. Or almost all, for it was
certainly evidence, said Davie to himself. The person who shoved the bag in the slot is the person who
handled the stone; don't forget that. Thinking which
he fell suddenly into one of his reveries; and yes, he
whispered, three minutes later, yes indeed. Then he
got up from the table and walked straight out of the
hotel into the street, turned to the right and presently entered Wonnacott's, the oldest established of
the Tidwell St. Peter's bakers.

It was still early. The shop was empty. Mrs. Wonnacott was arranging new loaves on a rack.

"Good morning, Mrs. Wonnacott," said Davie.

"Good morning, Dr. Davie." (Mrs. Wonnacott was
one of the few left in Tidwell St. Peter's who remembered Davie; they were of an age.)

"Do you deliver still, Mrs. Wonnacott?"

"Oh no," said Mrs. Wonnacott, "I'm afraid not.
My husband always delivered, but I've had to give it
up. You can't get the boys, and when you can, they
want too much money."

"I bet they do."

"Of course we take orders still, and I put them up

for the customers when they call. Were you wanting something, Dr. Davie?"

"Yes, please. I wanted to order half a dozen scones."

"Certainly."

"But not for today. Tomorrow."

"A pleasure, Dr. Davie. I'll mark a bag. Now let me see—tomorrow's the 8th, no 'tisn't, the 9th, that's right. Now"—and here she picked up a paper bag.

"How much?"

"Eighteen pence, please."

Davie planked the money down on the counter and watched Mrs. Wonnacott as she wrote in a corner of the bag with a stub of pencil.

There was no doubt about the writing. But she did not, he noticed, write "Paid," or "Pd." On the counter there were one or two other bags waiting to be filled, marked with their orders in the corner followed by abbreviated addresses—St M, Bal, Seav. None of these bore a "Pd," either.

"Thank you, Mrs. Wonnacott."

"Thank you, Dr. Davie. Another fine day, I do believe," said Mrs. Wonnacott.

As Davie walked back to the Ottery, he took the shabby paper out of his pocket and peered at it. "Those bags all have an address on them," he muttered, "but they're shortened. I've got to find out

what this word is. It looks like nothing, but it means
something. And, dear God!" he said, suddenly halting
at the foot of the steps. "Yes, I believe it does mean
something."

Dr. Davie bounded up the steps much quicker than
was good for him, pushed open the glass doors, and
approached the reception desk.

"Miss Mingo," he said, "could you oblige me—"

"If I can, Dr. Davie," said Miss Mingo. Obliging
people was just what she enjoyed. Miss Mingo aimed
to be a paragon among receptionists.

"I was wondering—have you such a thing as a magnifying glass? I hardly hope—"

"But I have, Dr. Davie," said Miss Mingo in high
feather.

"You have! You admirable person!"

Miss Mingo blushed a becoming pink. "Somebody
left a magnifying glass behind a year ago and never
claimed it, and I said 'I'll keep that. It will come in
useful one day.' Now let me see—"

Miss Mingo opened a drawer and ruffled around
in a conglomeration of pencils, sealing wax, string,
india rubbers, cellotape and scissors. "It's here somewhere, I know. Yes—here we are, Dr. Davie."

"You are a conjuror, Miss Mingo. I am most grateful. Some people's handwriting—"

"Oh yes!" said Miss Mingo, closing the drawer with
an air of achievement. "The letters we get making
reservations you'd never believe."

"I would, Miss Mingo."

Davie slipped the glass in his pocket and retired
to his bedroom. He had kept his end up with Miss
Mingo, but he felt slightly embarrassed with his own
company. He particularly disliked seeing himself in

the character of Holmes, but he needed that magnifying glass. For a full minute he stared through it at the writing on the paper bag. Then he opened a drawer and took out the newspaper report of the inquest which Giles had given him. He wanted to verify something.

That did not take long. Then he walked over to the window and sat down in that small uneasy chair peculiar to all provincial hotel bedrooms.

Like most people who live alone, Dr. Davie often talked to himself, not just inside his head, but out loud. He did so now. "One could never have hoped for anything to be so neat," he said. "The date, the bag, and the stone. *That* stone. I'm sure it's that stone. I knew I'd seen it before somewhere."

Pinewood. The stone and the bag had come from Pinewood. The last word began with a G, and it was Gonz. It meant Gonzago. And the 13th was the day that Adam Merrick died.

A robin alighted on the window sill and looked at Davie, with his head on one side. He seemed to have hopeful expectations. No doubt a former visitor had had proper views about crumbs. Davie liked robins, but he looked straight through this one. If I am right, he was thinking, it narrows it down from anybody to three. Surely I must be right. But what the devil does one do now?

II

His answer to that question was to climb the hill to Pinewood. It was impossible to go any further without talking to Mrs. Merrick. Basil Jason might be paying a farewell call before starting on his commercial travels. He hardly thought that would matter.

This time the front door did not stand open. It was early for callers—barely ten o'clock. But it made the business of ringing the bell more difficult. He almost wished he had not come. On the other side of the door he could hear a whirring noise. Someone was cleaning. Almost certainly it was not Mrs. Merrick.

For half a minute he waited. Then he disciplined himself and pushed the electric button, gently and briefly. It was an apology in advance. Immediately from within he heard that dying fall, that exhausted note, that helpless groan of a carpet sweeper deprived of breath, and then the door was opened by an amiable middle-aged woman wearing an apron. Behind her in the hall lay the serpentine involutions of her office.

"I am afraid I am rather early," said Davie, "but I wanted to catch Mrs. Merrick before she went out. Is she at home?"

"Yes, she is. If you'll come in, sir, I'll go and find her. I've just finished in the drawing room. You'll find it's all nice and tidy. What name shall I say?"

"Dr. Davie."

The woman shut the door. If then he had heard her going into the kitchen, or into the garden, he would have stood there waiting, probably stepping to the window to look through the pine trees to the sea. But she did not do either of these things; she stumped upstairs. If Mrs. Merrick were upstairs, thought Davie, she was probably doing intricate things to her face, and she would not come down until she was satisfied with the result. He also remarked that there were two steps on the stairs which creaked. In these circumstances (but marvelling a little at his own ill behaviour) he walked over to the Regency work table and opened the drawer. The colour photographs of the garden lay just where they had been before, the picture he had looked at longest still on top. He picked it up. Adam Merrick by the front door. A clump of daffodils to the right. The stone by the door. The stone with the curious white line across its diameter.

Two seconds was as much as he needed for that. Then he put the picture back, closed the drawer and strolled over to the window. Certainly it was the most splendid view. Certainly it was the most obvious place for a visitor to be found—and found he was only a second later. Mrs. Merrick trod with a lighter tread than Mrs. Merely. There had been no warning creak upon the stairs.

"Dr. Davie—good morning."

"I hope I'm not too early. I wanted to catch you before you joined the fashionable world in the village street."

"Do sit down. Have you had thoughts about the house?"

"I have had many. And I'm sorry to say I haven't resolved them."

"No?"

"Actually I'm calling to ask you about something different. And I find it embarrassing."

"Embarrassing? Does it concern my husband's death?"

"Yes, Mrs. Merrick, it does. You have gone straight to the point. I will do the same thing. Certain things have been forced on my notice. I wanted—"

"You do not altogether take me by surprise, Dr. Davie. I had heard that you had been showing an interest in my quarry. Why do you bother yourself about something the police and the coroner's jury were satisfied with? It only causes distress. I had much rather believe in an accident than the sort of thing you seem to be hinting at. You want to see me—about what?"

"That is the trouble, Mrs. Merrick. I am not a policeman. I am not trained to look for clues, make casts of footprints, decipher fingerprints. If I find a clue I am grateful. But in the main I can only think."

"And what have you thought?"

"I think that someone who had long had murderous designs on your husband was suddenly given an unlooked-for opportunity. I think that person heard a quarrel going on between him and Ernest Stubbings. It was growing dark. Mr. Merrick was about to go home by a path near the quarry, and he was in such a rage that he would probably be thinking only of his own irritations. He might therefore be easily surprised. I think that that person, knowing there was a large loose stone on the top of the gatepost of Rose Cottage, took that stone and waited near the path at a point where it was nearest to the quarry. I think that your husband was indeed slugged by this stone as he passed by, and that he staggered towards the edge and either fell or was pushed over."

"Surely you don't just spin these theories without any evidence?"

"Evidence: I agree—that is the rock which breaks the theorist. But there is evidence."

"There *is?*"

Then Davie told her about the stone he had found in the bracken. The stone with the girdle of mortar. The mortar which held three black human hairs. "The stone fits that cavity exactly; so there is one hard, undeniable fact. Someone took it from Mr. Parsley's gatepost. And someone put another stone in its place."

Davie paused and looked at Mrs. Merrick. But Mrs. Merrick was gazing steadily down at the carpet. It might have been that she considered the posture dramatically effective. Or it might have been that she disliked close scrutiny. She made no comment.

Davie leant forward in his chair, leaning his elbows on his knees.

"You remember our conversation about beach stones?"

"Yes, I do. You had views about not using them as doorstops."

"And so had you, I afterwards discovered."

Mrs. Merrick raised her eyes then. "How?"

"It isn't very long ago that you had one yourself—before you decided that the Elba stone was better looking."

"Yes, I did—but how on earth do you know when I started to use the Elba stone, or what I may have used before? You've only been here once."

Mrs. Merrick looked at him with amazement and amusement combined.

"Are you a wizard, Dr. Davie?"

"No. You told me yourself."

"*Told* you?"

"Yes—you said you had brought the Elba stones back two summers ago."

"Well?"

"And you showed me a picture of your husband standing beside the door in the spring. The daffodils were out, and he was beside them. And against the door was a beach stone. A recognizable stone, darker than some with a strange white line across the diameter. It came out well in the colour picture. You chose it, I expect, because it was unusual and dramatic-looking. What happened to it? An answer to that may lead us somewhere."

"I don't know where it is," said Mrs. Merrick, blushing a deep rose—and suddenly Davie remembered how, on his first visit, she had coloured, most becomingly coloured, when he had referred to the Elba stone at the door.

"Why? What happened to it?" he asked.

"I threw it away."

"Threw it away? When, Mrs. Merrick, when?" asked Davie eagerly, leaning forward.

"I don't know. It was cold weather after Adam died. No one in Tidwell St. Peter's was needing a doorstop—and after that I went away for a few days. It was some time about then."

"And you've never seen it since?"

"Never. What's so interesting about the stone?"

"Only this—that I think I've found it. I think it's the stone on Mr. Parsley's gatepost, the stone that took the place of the other one."

"This is fantastic."

"I agree. One wouldn't expect anyone to come here on purpose. But someone who knew the house, who lived nearby, who wanted a stone quickly—he might have taken it in an emergency, a dramatic emergency. Find that person—"

"What sort of person would do such a thing?"

"That's the point. Clues come to one by luck or by diligence. Speculation belongs to the mind. A person who kills a man with a stone is probably one who makes a sudden decision. He is no lurker with dagger or gun. He is one who seizes the unexpected opportunity. In this case he seems to have been one who loses his nerve in the end, who searches wildly for the weapon and defeats himself in the darkness, who makes a panic decision to substitute another stone—an unnecessary mistake; there are plenty of hooligans who spoil hedges and break gateposts. And, finally, the person must have acted quickly. Mr. Parsley does not seem to have noticed any substitution. He'd have noticed a gap. Which means that the stone must have been replaced early, before Mr. Parsley went out the next morning. By the way, you paid him an early call that day, so Mr. Parsley told me. I suppose you did not happen to notice—"

"No, I did not," said Mrs. Merrick. "I was not in a state of mind to notice absurd things like a stone on a gatepost."

Davie got up. "I mustn't bother you any longer, Mrs. Merrick. It was on my mind that I should be investigating things without your knowledge."

"Liar," said Mrs. Merrick to herself. To Davie she said, "Thank you for telling me. But I must say that I am by no means convinced by the things which you have told me. Especially about that stone. Nobody took it. I threw it away—down the slope. Who would go searching for it? It doesn't make sense."

"There was one other thing," said Davie quietly. "Is there any communication between your house and Miss Gonzago's small part of it?"

"None at all. It's cut off completely. Miss Gonzago has her own door. Is that of interest?"

Dr. Davie considered. Then, "Yes," he said, "it is— of very great interest. It means that on the night of March 13, or the early morning of March 14, you could not possibly have walked into her kitchen and borrowed a paper bag."

"No," said Mrs. Merrick. "I could not have done so. What is there significant in that?"

"Apparently nothing. I just wanted to know. Goodbye—and thank you for talking to me."

"Goodbye," said Mrs. Merrick, staring at him very hard. She did not see him to the door.

III

As he plodded back down the hill towards the village he was feeling a considerable fool. He had shown his hand and got absolutely nothing in return. Only an hour before he had been sure that he was moving in the right direction. Now he was asking himself if perhaps Rachel Merrick really had made that early morning call on Arthur Parsley merely in the character of the dramatic widow. It had seemed improbable. But then why (according to Ernest Stubbings) had Miss Gonzago called at Rose Cottage in the middle of the night? Doubtless, an exaggeration; but why had she called at all? And where did Arthur Parsley come into this tangled story? Arthur Parsley . . .

Originally the thing that had interested him about Arthur Parsley had been that modern snowstorm, not anything to do with the death of Adam Merrick. He had been led into these further speculations.

Towards the bottom of the hill there are a few shops: yet another antique business, a tobacconist, a dairy. Behind the glass door of the dairy a poster was stuck. The Horticultural Society announced its late summer flower show in the Parish Hall. Davie stopped for a moment and read about it. And "Dear God!" he said (for the second time that day), "Dear God! I'd forgottten the Horticultural Society. Now that makes *another* difference. Everything I've been thinking about, *everything* is just slightly out all along the line. My arguments have been like a set of photographs all slightly out of focus. They're nearly right, but not right enough. The Horticultural Society is important. And I'd left it out altogether."

When he got to the village street, he hesitated. He had not meant to do it. But now there seemed no alternative. He would have to ask Miss Gonzago about that snowstorm.

A few large drops of rain began to fall as he turned into Fore Street, and as though by prearrangement the passwords altered automatically. "Is it the end of summer?" they gaily asked each other. And "There's going to be a cloudburst any moment now," said the more facetious ones, as they hurried on their way.

Coming out of Wonnacott's was a little spare woman with an armful of parcels.

"Good morning, Dr. Davie," she said. "I'm Mrs. Stubbings—remember?"

"Yes, indeed," said Davie. "I'm sorry I didn't recognize you. You're wearing a hat."

"Ah," said Mrs. Stubbings, mysteriously. "That's Mr. Stubbings. As wife to the chairman, he says—" And suddenly convulsed by some internal merriment, she moved in the direction of home. "It's going to rain like one o'clock," said Mrs. Stubbings over her shoulder.

An old-fashioned bell on a spring aroused itself to a frenzy as he opened Miss Gonzago's door. There was no one else in the shop. Davie adjusted his tie in an eighteenth-century glass, and looked around him. There was no specialization here, but plenty to like. Samplers, plates with "Thou God Seest Me" on them, a mug from Queen Victoria's jubilee, a collection of fans, a leash of Staffordshire dogs. It was the sort of shop where you might find anything, and the first thing that Davie found was a Worcester cup, Dr. Wall period certainly, white and fluted, with a royal blue band edged with gold. He might be obliged to buy that, he was thinking; and then suddenly he realized that he was not alone any longer. Miss Gonzago was standing at the back of the shop in a doorway, watching him, almost shyly, he might have thought, if his heart had not already prejudged the situation. As it was, it seemed to Davie that she was watching him as he was watching her.

"Good morning. I was looking at your pretty things," said Davie,

"Please do."

"And I wanted, if I may, to ask you a question. I'm a bit of a collector myself and I'm very attached to snowstorms. You know what I mean?"

"Indeed, yes," said Miss Gonzago. "We had one in

our nursery. My brother broke it, I remember, because he wanted to find out how it worked. And then of course it wouldn't. I've always been rather fond of them. I wish I had one to show you, but I haven't."

"Mr. Parsley," Davie plunged on, "I expect you know him—"

"Yes, indeed."

"Mr. Parsley very kindly showed me his excellent collection. And among them there was a modern one, done in some cheap material, which I thought singular. He said he'd been given it, but that it had come from your shop."

Miss Gonzago blushed a little, as she said, "Yes, I remember."

"Might I ask you where you got it from?"

Davie looked full at Miss Gonzago, and Miss Gonzago looked back at him.

"I'm so sorry," she said like one condoling with the bereaved. "But I don't know. It sounds silly but it's true. Actually I *found* it. I'm fond of flowers, wild ones as well as garden ones, and I often go out botanizing. One day I went to the old sandstone quarry to see what I could find. I'm sure one isn't supposed to go in, but it looked so mysterious and inviting, and I did. And it was worth it. For one thing, there was a privet hawk moth sitting on a log, and you don't see that every day. And then there was this thing on the edge of a rubbish dump. And, really, I thought, I can't just let that be thrown away. So I popped it in my basket and brought it home. It seemed new, and I suppose I was stealing—it must have got there by accident—but I don't like needless destruction."

"No, nor do I," said Davie. "But I fear you aren't going to find me another one."

"I'm afraid not."

"I'm sorry I've bothered you," said Davie, setting a course for the door. "That's a pretty Dr. Wall cup."

"Ah—you do think it is Dr. Wall?"

"Certainly. That glorious blue. That fluting. Goodbye. I must hurry. It's going to rain."

Miss Gonzago stood at her door for a minute and watched him as he made his way back up the street towards the Ottery.

"I'm sure he doesn't really want that snowstorm," she said to herself. "So why does he ask about it?"

"A letter for you, Dr. Davie," said Miss Mingo at the reception desk. "Second post."

A letter from London. He did not recognize the hand. He took it into the sun lounge. Before opening it he sat there for a minute watching the rain battering on the large windows. Certainly the fine weather had broken.

It was a letter from Donald, with a postscript from Irene. He read it over three times. Then he put it in his pocket. He would answer it after luncheon. Just at the moment he did not want to be disturbed. The truth, he felt sure of it, was only just round the corner. But somehow he had got himself into a muddle. The only thing to do was to go back a bit and think again. He took out the blue notebook. There were not many pages left now. But writing was the only way to secure his thoughts.

MRS. MERRICK [he wrote]. I meant to surprise
her with my question about the bag. She was
not surprised. Just bewildered. I meant to surprise her about the stone. She just did not believe me. It *is* a bit steep. How can one identify
a stone from a photograph? Was she putting up
a good performance, or was I on totally wrong
lines?

The vital thing is the bag. Gonz. Gonzago. It
was surely Miss Gonzago's to begin with. But I'd
assumed Mrs. Merrick could have borrowed it.
Perhaps she didn't. It's easier if she didn't. But
the alternative seemed so improbable. Miss Gonzago . . .

And there he suddenly stopped, uncertain what to
write next. There was so much of it. He was thinking again of Miss Gonzago's little picnic, of his own
half-waking fantasy of the early morning, of Miss
Gonzago's strange explanation of the snowstorm. And
then his mind switched, and he was thinking about
Mrs. Wonnacott and her paper bags.

After which he looked out of the window for two
or three minutes.

Presently, through the extraordinary telegraphy of
mental association, he found himself recalling the
plot of an old thriller he had long ago admired. He'd
forgotten what it was called or who wrote it. He'd
forgotten if it were a full story or a short story. He'd
forgotten most of it, indeed, except one central fact.
It was about a man who killed a visitor from Aus-
tralia, a one night visitor, killed him, stole his money,
buried him in the garden and built a rockery over

him. It was neatly done. The killer was safe as con-
crete—except for one little trouble. He could not
leave the garden alone. He had to be there. He had
to be gardening. Then there came a detective who
asked questions, and somehow discovered the secret—
how Davie had entirely forgotten. The one thing he
remembered was the man and the rockery. He was
a chemist, he suddenly remembered; and he'd poisoned the chap.

That was the story, often remembered, long admired, which came into his head and flew away again
while he sat staring at a blank page and thinking
about Seaview and Balmoral and St. Mary's and Blue-
bells and Kosy Kot, and all the rest of Mrs. Wonnacott's abbreviated clientele—which included, he now
recorded with a smile, the eccentric Mrs. Stubbings.

And then, "Ass, purblind and credulous ass," he
said to himself, suddenly shutting up the blue notebook and putting it in his pocket. Goodness, he had
been stupid! . . .

Hauling himself out of his chair, he went down
the passage and rang up Giles.

"It's like one of those quiz questions," he told himself as he waited for an answer to his ring. "Which
is the odd man out? Ah, hullo—is that you, Giles?"

"Yes."

"I think I may have discovered the answer to our
problems."

"You *have*?"

"We could have a chance of making certain tonight, if you wouldn't mind joining me in a small
burglary."

"At what hour?" said Giles. He enjoyed playing it
cool as much as Davie did.

"Come to dinner, bringing with you as many keys as you can lay hands on. Keys for a padlock. A modern padlock. Can you do that?"

"I think so. You mean the padlock on—"

"Yes," said Davie, "that one."

IV

It had rained all the afternoon. Davie had slept, and read, and written a letter to Irene. He would be back in London in three or four days' time, he told her, and if she were still at the Dorset he would come to see her.

After tea he went for a walk. The rain had stopped, but the clouds hung fixed as in a picture, hardly moving across the sky. There was scarcely anyone in the street. The shops were beginning to shut; it was not yet opening time for the pubs.

As he neared Turpin's, Miss Gonzago came out of the shop, clutching a loaf of bread. She crossed the road to the post office with a handful of letters. "What a day! What a day!" she said to an old lady on the pavement, and the old lady made some whimsical retort about Noah's ark. Then Miss Gonzago climbed up the terrace behind the church, a road which would take her to Pinewood.

He did not go on up West Hill. He had had enough of West Hill. Instead he turned to the left and walked up a steep terrace of Victorian houses, leading to a pine wood and the cliffs. The sea was rough, grey and deserted. There were no bathers. The boats were drawn up high on the beach. A few gulls swung through the air in disapproving parabolas. But most of them had flown inland to strut about absurdly in the fields. It was a sure sign of the weather when the gulls did that. The evening would be dark.

The evening would be dark. He did not feel happy about what he meant to do in it. But he thought about K. W. Myrtle and knew that he had to do it.

Then he walked down the cliff path to the Ottery and waited for Giles.

V

It was eleven o'clock when they left the hotel. "We'll walk," Davie had said. "It's not very far, and it saves parking."

When they reached the quarry, it was quite dark. There was a lamp near the brook which cast a faint illumination on the gate and on the ancient crooked notice board in the elder bush. But inside the quarry it was midnight black, silent as the bottom of the sea and nearly as wet. Water dropped from the branches over their heads, water brushed from the grasses and brambles. The path was slippery with mud.

"I don't want to use the torch much," Davie had said to Giles before they started, and twice he lost the path among the nettles, before they found the shed suddenly in front of them, black against black.

"Here we are," said Giles quietly. "And there's Maison Stubbings." Davie peered through the darkness and saw two lighted windows, one unshaded on the ground floor, one shaded, above it. "Mrs. Stubbings has gone to bed," said Giles.

"You said you thought Stubbings couldn't see the floor of the quarry from there," said Davie. "He can —not all of it, of course—but some of it. I took particular note of that when I was in the garden."

" 'On such a night as this,' " Giles said, "I should hope he can't see a thing."

"Try those keys."

"Can I have a light once?"

"No."

"All right. I'll try without."

Then he set to work, and Davie heard him saying, "No—no—no—no—blast! I've dropped it—no—no . . ."

He said "No" eleven times.

"What about the one you dropped?"

"Can I put the light on?"

"You must."

At first he could not see it, but it had to be there. Kneeling in the mud, he bent back the weeds and found it hiding under a plantain leaf.

"Wipe it," said Davie, and stood there in the darkness expecting the word "No." But instead he heard a click. "Got it," whispered Giles.

"Put the padlock in your pocket with the key," said Davie. Then he heard the door creak backwards like a forbidden secret in Bluebeard's castle, and felt the rough wood against his hand.

"We'll have to use the light in here," said Giles. "Come on."

"Shade it as much as you can."

Covering the torch with his handkerchief, Giles shone it slowly around the shed, rousing and losing shadows as he turned about. Near the door there were shovels and pickaxes. They were rusty; it did not look as though the Tidwell St. Peter's councilmen had often been asked to handle them. On a shelf on the far side of the shed were some wooden boxes. They were locked. On the floor below the shelf were two larger cases. Giles went down on his knees. "These are open," he said quietly. He lifted the lid of one of the cases and peered inside. Leaning over his shoulder Davie could see nothing, but he heard him suddenly whisper, "Well, I'll be damned!"

"What is it?"

"There's a lot of those cheap snowstorms here, like the one Arthur has."

"Give me one," said Davie. "That's what I wanted. Now we can go."

Giles handed it up. Davie put it in his pocket. There was no light and no time to examine it.

"Can't I look in the other one?"

"Well—just a glance." Then, "No," Davie whispered. "Put the light out. And don't move."

Somewhere on the path he had heard a sound. Not a hard sound. Not a sound made by a foot on a stone. The grass and the mud were soft. It was the light swish of material against a branch. Then silence.

Thoughts rushed through Davie's head. The person who at this hour of night, and at this inconvenience, was coming to protect his own would not be gentle. There was too much at stake for that. He would be armed. Davie had no weapon. The shovels and picks were out of reach. Anyhow they'd be useless against a gun. He waited.

And then a light stabbed through the darkness and held him. Behind it in the doorway stood a small figure wearing a black mackintosh. Its face was hidden in a black nylon stocking. Its hand held a revolver.

There was no hope in this situation except one. The light pinned Davie to the wall like a biological specimen. But its narrow beam did not encompass Giles, kneeling under the shelf two yards away.

And then the figure in the doorway spoke. It was impossible to say if he recognized the voice, it said so little. It said, "Come out."

There was nothing else to be done. He came out. Then the voice said, "Walk." From behind him the torch pointed the way he was to go. It was the path towards the deep side of the pool. The conclusion was obvious.

Soundless on the grass, Giles took the black body from behind, his left arm round the neck, the right pinning the revolver arm. It was all over in five seconds. As Davie turned round he saw the two figures slip in the mud. For a second the light shone upwards, sharply illuminating a branch of sycamore. Then suddenly it was dark, and he heard the torch spinning against a tree trunk.

And then the sound of running steps. The figure in black was trying to get away, and Giles was stumbling after it.

It was no good Davie following them. He stood there in the darkness listening. The steps had run across the open part of the quarry and then faded away on the grass on the further side. From there the person might take the private path to Pinewood, or the public path, or the shortest cut round the top of the quarry. That would lead to the road and perhaps to a waiting car. Or to refuge in Cadleigh woods.

At first he could hear nothing. Then faintly but certain, he heard running steps above him. The black mackintosh was making for the high road. If it got there, it would probably get away. And Giles would probably get shot.

In the last few minutes it had grown lighter in the quarry. A rising wind had blown the clouds apart, and in the cleft a watery moon peered like some picture in a Gothic novel. In that dramatic setting he stood waiting for a sound. And the sound that he heard was a sudden slithering noise and a great cry. And a splash.

In the faint light he could see something dark and new at the shallow end of the water. Pray God it isn't Giles! he thought—and added in his logical way, but it's no use praying God. Either it is or it isn't.

As fast as he could, he made his way round the edge of the pool. And then, as he neared the darkness in the water, the clouds drew together again. The darkness was everywhere. He could see nothing. "Giles!" he called softly.

The quarry had a way with sound. "Giles!" It was enough.

"Dr. Davie! Where are you?" Above him on the precipice a torch flashed.

"Down by the water."

"Hold on—I'm coming."

For a minute he watched the torch bobbing its way down the edge of the quarry. Then Giles was beside him shining the light on the pond.

Flat on its back, in not more than a foot of murky water, lay the figure in the black mackintosh. And at its feet, like some surrealist memorial to the dead, the spokes of the umbrella pointed to the sky.

Giles took off his shoes and socks, rolled up his trousers, splashed through the water and brought the dark object to land.

"I told you whom I expected to unmask," said Davie quietly. "But the term was figurative. I did not expect we would really have to do that. Draw it back. Or, if you like, I will."

"It's all right," said Giles. "I'll do it."

Then slowly and delicately and decently he rolled back the nylon stocking, and they looked down at the dead face of Ernest Stubbings.

VI

Four days later Davie was having tea with Irene in her rooms at the Dorset Hotel. Donald was out.

"How did you get there?" Irene asked.

"Not by the swift exercise of intelligence," said Davie. "I made endless mistakes. First I thought it was Mrs. Merrick—in collaboration with Jason. This was because of the stone, and because of her early morning visit to Arthur Parsley. I couldn't understand why she hadn't telephoned. I thought the visit was an excuse to replace the stone."

"You'd not allowed for Rachel Merrick's sense of drama."

"Exactly. Then I was sure it was Miss Gonzago, because of the stone, because of her night visit to Arthur Parsley, because of her picnic, and because—

because most of all—of the bag. For a while I even suspected Arthur Parsley—most harmless of men—because of his connection with Miss Gonzago. It was days before I remembered that there had been a committee meeting of the Horticultural Society on the night of March thirteenth. Miss Gonzago never made a midnight call at Rose Cottage. She was leaving a late meeting—and I don't suppose it was as late as Stubbings chose to make out.

"I suspected Parsley again when I found RTK 549H parked near his gate. But of course Jason only left it there because he didn't want to leave it outside Stubbings's house. It takes so little to put one on the wrong trail.

"But the deciding evidence was the paper bag. Of course I took Gonz to stand for Gonzago—until suddenly I realized a glaring discrepancy, an odd-man-outness in Mrs. Wonnacott's shorthand. Gonzago was a *person's* name. All the other names, Bal and St. M., were the names of *houses*. And so of course was Gonz. It stood for Gonville—I had persuaded myself to make a Z out of a V. Gonv was Gonville Lodge, late Quarry View, residence of Ernest Stubbings. And, to clinch that, I discovered that Mrs. Stubbings shopped at Wonnacott's, while Miss Gonzago (and Mrs. Merrick) went to Turpin's."

"You clever old thing," said Irene.

"Not a bit clever. I'd been uncommonly silly. In conjunction with the bag I had to alter my mind about that damned stone. I'd been too smart about that. A stone with a white girdle is uncommon, but it's not unique. The stone and the bag had to go together. It came from Gonville Lodge, and I don't doubt that Stubbings dug up some of his own daffodils to cover its disappearance. It was silly of him."

"So Stubbings was running the drugs as he ran everything else in Tidwell St. Peter's. And Adam Merrick thought he could outsmart him."

"Yes, but it wasn't a desire to solve Merrick's death that made me go on with this. It was nothing to me who killed him. I was concerned with something much more important—the life of a boy in my college, the lives of other boys. I was convinced there was a connection between the snowstorm at Cambridge and the snowstorm at Rose Cottage. The difficulty was to find out about the Parsley snowstorm without arousing suspicion. I had no way of knowing whom not to speak to about it. But I did know from Donald that Merrick had been mixed up in drug smuggling. I thought a trade rival would be more likely to have killed him than a lover or a guilty wife. Find a murderer and unmask a dope smuggler, I thought, or find a dope smuggler and unmask a murderer.

"In the end the affair in the quarry resulted partly from something Miss Gonzago told me, and partly from a half-remembered story. A man can guard a secret too closely. There was something odd about Ernest Stubbings's interest in that quarry. And something odd about his connection with Basil Jason, commercial traveller, and with Walter Ford, fisher for lobsters; Walter Ford, whose earrings glistened in the night as he carried two cases into Basil Jason's house. You don't absolutely need a motorboat to go lobster fishing. You don't fish for lobsters in midchannel. So I took a chance. It could all have been an empty mistake. But as it happened, it wasn't."

"There was no case for the police last March," said Irene, "and now—"

"And now there is, and most of it has been found in the boot of RTK 549H. It's strange to think that all this springs from the blue notebook which I found in the library drawer."

Irene looked down at the carpet.

"On the day of Robert's funeral," she said quietly.

Then she looked up at Davie and told him what she had been unable to write in her letter.

"R.V. Please don't think me a terrible woman. I did love Robert. I loved him very much. If Robert had lived I don't know what would have happened. Divorce, I suppose. But, now that he's dead we couldn't help ourselves. Donald and I *had* to marry. I could not allow my child to be the wrongful heir to Cadleigh. Please say you understand."

"My dear," said Davie. "You are the most honest girl I ever met. Robert knew what he was doing when he married you."